GREAT BRITISH HORROR IV

DARK AND STORMY NIGHTS

Great British Horror IV
Dark and Stormy Nights

Edited by
Steve J Shaw

BLACK
SHUCK
BOOKS

First published in Great Britain in 2019 by

Black Shuck Books
Kent, UK

978-1-913038-44-1

In memory of Charles Black

Nor Cease You Never Now

Ren Warom

It was a dark and stormy night...

Is that how they want it to start? All these flashcards. These prompts and pieces of paper. *Fictionalise it,* they say, *tell it as a story to find some distance.* But who'd start a story like that? Nonsensical. Self-evident. Night tends to be dark. Why would it not be? The light is gone. The world has turned away from sun, from warmth – submerged in the darkness of space. Anyway, it's irrelevant, because it wasn't night, and there was no storm.

There was only water.

There's no story, either, only fragments scattered all around. Memory is particular and arbitrary. So is trauma. Attach trauma to memory and it chooses what it will cling to at random – but with intent. Witness a car crash whilst eating strawberry ice cream, all those bodies burst like fruit and leaking, and the thought of strawberry ice cream might make you sick for the rest of your life – particular and yet arbitrary. She's not afraid of the obvious, of water. If anything, she's drawn to it. Hypnotised.

She can eat a steak rare, too, and feel nothing. That shocks her parents. They watch her when she's eating, expecting the reaction Luke had – maybe because they're

9

twins or something. Luke's gone vegan. He'll look at meat, look at people eating meat, and go *pale*, swallow like he's fighting the urge to throw up. Memory lives in meat for him. For her though, it's her face. She can't see herself at all. Her face has been stolen by trauma. So there it is... Arbitrary. Particular.

In which case, what use are stories?

What use is anything?

❖

s   d   r   d   o   i

Luke's in the back of the corner shop, trying to decide between buying a whole lemon cake or three packs of bourbons. He keeps doing this, spending money on unhealthy crap, food with too much sugar and flavourings, anything to try and erase the taste of meat clinging to his tongue, to the back of his throat. He overhears voices, talking a little too loud. Purposeful.

"Disgusting. I can't believe he's walking around like this. It's blatant."

"I can't believe they let that family buy the cottage in the first place. Bad for the area, it is. For house prices."

"Does Geoff say so?"

"He does. I mean, it's still all over the news, especially with them moving. Especially with that awful accident on the day they moved... It can't be a coincidence."

"No."

"I mean, look at what happened. They still don't know why that boat capsized. How those two managed to survive. The *only* ones to come out of the water."

"Too much of a coincidence."

"Exactly. *Exactly*. But do the police do anything?"

"Not likely, they leave us to be around *that*. I won't let my kids stay at the college if they attend, I can tell you that."

"I don't blame you, love, I don't blame you."

Luke *hates* these people. These women and men with their gossip and their curiosity. Their malice. They know he's here, listening, they saw him come in, watched him trail to the back of the shop. They mean for him to hear this. To hurt him. He never realised how *ugly* people could be. That urge they have to poke and worry at something already cracked and leaking. The will to believe the worst, to want it. The hunger for drama. For horror. He thinks of the accident on the motorway. The blackened ruin, the collapse of cars behind; the way people slowed down to look.

It's amazing how fast suffering can pull an enthusiastic crowd. How fast a crowd can turn, screaming for blood.

If they knew the taste of it, the price, maybe they wouldn't.

"Well," one of the voices says, and the sharpness in it is malice and satisfaction both, "they fit in out there, at least, in the sticks. Out on the fens. They say the people of the fens didn't go hungry during the war, during rationing. How do you think they did that?"

There's a shocked, almost delighted silence, and then the other one goes, "Oh my god, Jess!"

"I said it, and I'd say it again."

He leaves without cake. Without biscuits. Without

looking at them. Goes home in silence, swallowing again and again at the taste in his mouth. Bitter and strong it spreads all the way down to his stomach, where it wraps around the meat of him and sinks in deep, reminding him that he'll never get rid of the taste of her. She's an accusation built into his body. A memory like a stain, and he's soaked through. Sodden with her.

❖

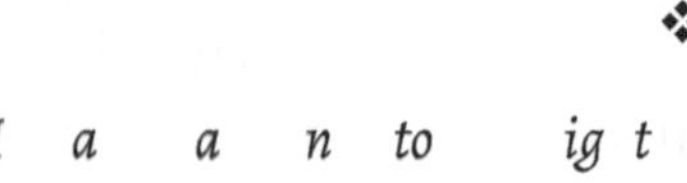

"*Fuck's* sake, what's this?"

Luke, in the passenger seat, his whole body will be tensing forward, as if ready to jump. Driving, Jay will tense too, barely perceptible – he'll want to say something about Luke's language but the words will stick in his throat. They've forgotten how to parent. Is that fear? What is that? In the middle row, Clara will reach out a hand to touch Luke's shoulder but pause, fingers curling on the air, as his eyes catch hers in the rearview.

The car slows to a crawl, then stops. In the back seats, the last row of three, lying down, Laurel's been watching the green blur of the banks roll to sky and cloud and back again. When they stop, she doesn't bother sitting up to see what's happening. Knowing makes no difference.

"It's a car accident." Clara, on her phone. For her, knowing is safety, despite all evidence to the contrary. "Seventeen cars!" She gasps. "Oh my god. This is a twenty-mile tailback."

"Can't we go around?" Luke's knee is jittering now, it's shaking the car.

Jay answers, deep and quiet, in control. Or so he thinks. "We could try, but the next junction is about eighteen miles. Then it's at least a half hour drive to get back to the motorway, and I'd guess we wouldn't be the only ones thinking to do that…"

"Shit." The impatience in Luke's voice trips on an edge. He's full of edges.

Clara butts in, conciliatory, voice like syrup, sickly sweet, all calories and no substance. "There's services in five miles. We can check in there for food. Coffee. Make it fun?"

"Cool, cool." Luke doesn't sound like he thinks it's cool, but he won't say more, not with Jay there. Jay will only tolerate so much. That's not parenting, that's just human. Everyone has a breaking point.

Clara leans over the back of her seat. "Hey, Lau, sound cool?" She's all but whispering, always tiptoeing around their feelings.

"Whatever." Miles away, she barely recognises her own voice. She wonders if she'd know her own face right now. Faces fall off. They change.

It takes three hours to get to the services, another hour to get back out. By the time they're back in traffic, Luke's retreated to his headphones, Jay having finally, *finally* lost his cool with Luke's lack of it, and the car is all tension, thick and ugly. For the past hour the view's been nothing but sky, slowly turning grey. There's a tiny patch of white adrift in the middle, fading fast. As it goes the first drops come, like Morse code. SOS.

Laurel lies in the back seat, counting seconds by her heartbeat, her skin thrumming like the metal skin of a car revved too hard. Morse code spatters multiply to a roar, reducing visibility to almost nil, the window a ragged blur of monochrome greys and the spreading yellow haloes of motorway lights. She doesn't want to be here.

She didn't want to come at all.

❖

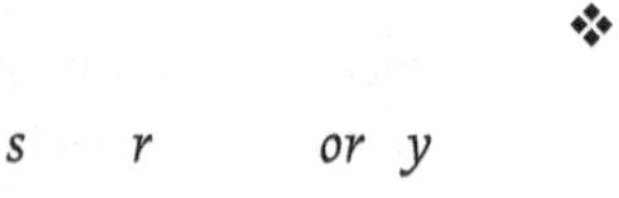

They both feel it, the rising tide. The call of water. It's been building within, like the quieting shushing of waves across pebbles, that rhythmic to and fro, the pull and release and pull again, until every scrap of sand, no matter how hard it clings together, is pulled apart and washed away. Even when they understand what it might cost, they can't resist the pull of it, the disintegration. It's like an apology. An offering. One they wouldn't refuse even if they could. The water almost had them once, and it's never really let go. That's why they came here, where the memory of water soaks the earth. Dominates it.

Water has called them here. It has claimed them. And when it comes to take them, it will find them sleeping and fill their lungs to brimming.

❖

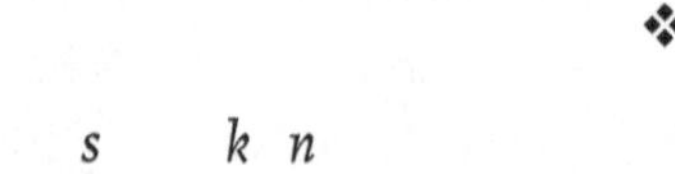

You try not to give too much of yourself away, hold on to the parts that matter, that feel right, but you end up losing them anyway. Bit by bit, the world steals you away from yourself, leaving you with scraps. Too few pieces, so you forget how to put them back together to make something, anything, resembling you, or who you thought you were. Who you wanted to be. There's just a shadow. A stranger. An outline that loses all resolution until it fades into nothing, into the surrounding dark, and is gone.

Lau stares into the mirror, her eyes pools of black in the darkness, her mouth a circle bleeding into her face. A chasm. She knows the truth now.

The face she almost swallowed was her own.

w   d r n o

It's Sunday. Seven weeks, four boxes remaining, all theirs. All left outside their rooms. An unspoken expectation from their parents to move in, move on. They've been mentioning college, leaving prospectuses around. When they go to work, Luke tears them up and throws them in the bin, mainly to stop Lau burning them. They know they won't be going back. Not now. Maybe never. Nothing is the same, and it can't be. It can't. On the screen, his character shoots and runs, runs and shoots. Mindless, his fingers press buttons automatically. He used to be good at this. He used to be a lot of things.

Laurel enters from the kitchen, shoes dangling from one hand. There are circles under her eyes he'd probably have given her shit for once upon a time, when she'd have cared. When he would. Heading to the front door, shoes swinging, she stops to pull them on, and then opens it. Pauses on the threshold without looking back. It hasn't happened for a long time. Knowing. But it happens now. He gets up from the sofa, dropping the controller behind him, barely hearing the thump of it on the floor. Takes her hand at the door, almost dragging. She laughs then, a small sound, like relief more than joy, more than anything.

"Where we going?" He's leading, but he asks her.

In response she moves to lead.

"I've been dreaming of faces," she says, tugging lightly on his hand. Her palm is cold. Damp. "Faceless people."

He swallows, walking faster. "We said we wouldn't say. You made me swear."

"I can break a fucking swear if I want to." Stubborn. This is the Laurel he knows. It's almost reassuring.

"Can you?" No bite in it. He's not arguing, not yet. Temper has faded lately, swallowed by fear. By something darker. A will to drown.

"I know why you went vegan, Luke," she says, so quiet and firm he turns his head to look at her. Her face is solemn. "I was in the water too," she adds, as if he needs reminding.

"That's why we promised, isn't it?"

She shrugs. "Maybe. Probably."

"So?"

"So what are you seeing?"

He doesn't reply until they reach their destination. A miniature wood in the midst of a large furrowed field, a small pond hidden within, and a fallen tree, partially rotted. This was an island once, surrounded by mirror-smooth waters all the way to the horizon, reflecting the sky. It must have been surreal, sky on all sides, above and below. You could jump and think you might float away, only to fall in and drown.

He's been here, so many times. It's like a call, a pull, the same as this twin thing they have, as if that water, or the memory of it, has magnetised him. He's found himself wandering here when he's intended to go to the shop, when he walks just to move and not feel like he might burst apart. They sit on the fallen tree, side by side, hand in hand, and watch the sky, bright blue, ripe with thick cumulus, drifting.

"I ate her," he says, then, like a confession.

"Katie?" She says the name in a rush, but it still hurts. It's Lau though, so he forgives it. Nothing else to do.

"Yeah."

"You're seeing her then."

"Sometimes. In the mist. But mostly I choke her up. Little pieces of her. And then they vanish."

She turns to look at him. "Where do they go?"

"Back inside," he says, and feels something moving in his gut, a tangle of viscera not his own. Foreign matter. "They go back inside."

a d   k   r

It's the usual breakfast in their half-finished kitchen, the cabinets painted varying shades of grey because Clara can't decide which is most sophisticated, and the crappy thrifted table. She insists she'll upcycle it, but the cloth she put down to sand and paint it is still under their feet, and the table hasn't been touched. That's how things are. Untouched. Unchanged. Or changed in awkward ways that stand out too fresh and raw to ignore. Their children are not getting better. He can't say it aloud and neither can she, but they exchange awareness of it when they look at one another. Over breakfast, at bedtime, on the sofa. Things are worse. Everything is dark, and everyone is drowning.

❖

That's how I remember it... muddled. Not just that day, but everything. I used to have this clear timeline, and it's gone. They're like *he has anger issues*, and yeah, I do, I lose my shit all the time. But it's not *them*. It's not their fault. I get mad because nothing stays where it should. Nothing makes *sense*. Not just memory, but everything. Everything. It's all shadows. You know how shadows get distorted? How they don't look like the thing they're made from?

Her family posted photos to their Facebook, you know. I kept going to look at them, but I don't know who that is, that girl. I didn't really know her at all. I mean, I didn't try for that. I wouldn't have. She was sweet, and quiet, and made it easy to be... I made her life fucking miserable okay? Because it was *easy*. That's what I did. That's how she knew me. I was the arsehole who made her cry pretty much every day at school.

That was her memory, and now she's gone.

And all I can think of, when I think of her, is that I *ate* her. And they tell me that it was an accident, that it might not have been her at all, not when so many of them... not with so many remains in the water. But that's all I can think of, and that it's not her, in those pictures. They're a lie.

All of this is a fucking lie.

❖

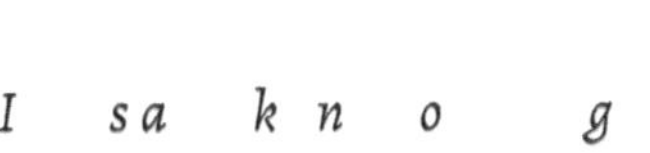

If I imitate the reflection, I will become the image, she thinks, resting her hand lightly on the surface of the water. Breaking it. Her face stares back at her as the ripples smooth out to a mirror. Nothing has changed. Water, mirror, it makes no difference, her image is blurred, a fuzz of colour and darkness where her features should be. She can't make it come to focus, as if a soft and constant rain is falling on the water, disturbing the surface tension. Water upon water. Water into water. That makes sense. It's all water, always.

In the mirrored surface, her reflection ripples and vanishes, replaced by bland blue sky. Lurching up, she stumbles back blindly, reaching for something, anything. But there's nothing to hold onto. Everything has vanished.

❖

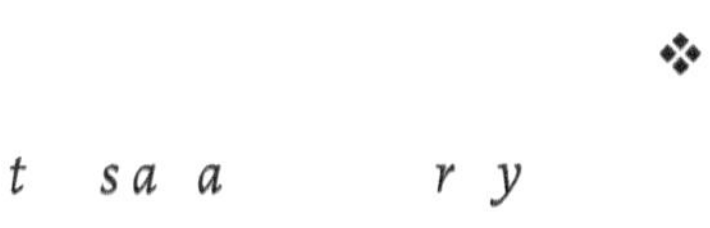

"Tell me what you're feeling. I'm not here to judge. Everything said in this room is in confidence."

Clara smiles, a touch uneasy. She clears her throat, looking at Jay for support, he reaches over and grabs hold of her hand, squeezing. Nods.

"It's just," she starts, then stops, looking down at her hands, her shoulders hitching once, and then again. When she speaks again, her voice is thick, heavy. "You get your children back, but they're no longer your children, you know? And... and you don't know what to do with these traumatised strangers, and they're, oh my god, just *breaking your heart*. I look at them and I *ache*. I don't have a clue how to help them, or what to say, and I'm scared of pushing them. I think... that would be bad."

"Jay?" Amanda, their bereavement and trauma counsellor, looks at Clara's husband and presses gently, "Do you feel the same?"

"I..." His jaw tenses. "I don't know how I feel. Helpless? I keep looking at them and wondering where Luke and Laurel are."

"That's perfectly understandable." Amanda looks between them, her face filled with compassion. "Trauma can have a profound impact on a personality. They're grieving, dealing with almost dying, with surviving, with the particular horrors of that survival. They'll improve, but it will take time, and patience, a great deal of patience. Normality is the best medicine you can offer them. Let them know nothing has changed, that there is stability they can trust."

"I try that. I do," Clara says. "But, I look at them, and I find myself wondering sometimes... would it be better if they'd died? And then I wonder if they can tell I'm thinking it and I feel so guilty, so *awful*. Like I've betrayed them."

The second it's out there, in the open, she's horrified to have said it, her hand over her mouth, her eyes wide, staring at Jay. He smiles, and it's painful. Lifts her hand to his mouth and kisses it.

"I think it," he says, softly. "I think it, too."

❖

They've been here a week, and he's spent most of it out of the house, unable to bear himself, the way he snaps at anything and everything. How it makes them react. The tension flooding the house is his doing, he drags it with him like a tidal wave, washing away any chance of peace. Even Lau won't speak to him half the time, but maybe that's not his temper. He's lost the ability to be calm, she's lost the ability to care. He's walking the roads between the fields today, he likes the endless emptiness of it all, how it stretches on forever, dragging the eye with it to hazy distance merging into sleepy blue sky. It makes him feel.

He's stopped to breathe it all in when she appears on the horizon, flickering in the heat haze like a ghost. Her hand is rested lightly on the rail, her hair blowing behind her, a tangle of agitated brown. She's laughing with her friends, holding back her hair as it whips into her mouth. Minutes later – or was it seconds? – their laughter turned to screams as a whining, grinding roar came from below, the boat pitching, sudden and steep, water splashing over the rails. Their whole class was there, some in the cabin, some on the deck.

Everyone on the deck died, apart from him and Laurel.

He watches as Katie and her friends tumble down, hitting the waves with violent slaps of sound. They fell together, churned to pieces by the engine blades as they spun through the water. He slid down the deck after them, hands scrabbling for purchase. He remembers the cold shock of the water, the screams, the blades spinning over his head in slow motion, the force of their movement pushing him down in a whirlpool of remains. Hers. He had no idea he would scream until it happened, and when he opened his mouth, she flooded inside, coppery and warm.

He rubs his hands over his eyes. When he looks again, she's back on the horizon. This time her gaze is on him, and when the wind whips her hair into her mouth, she doesn't reach to pull it away. She opens wide, and swallows it.

❖

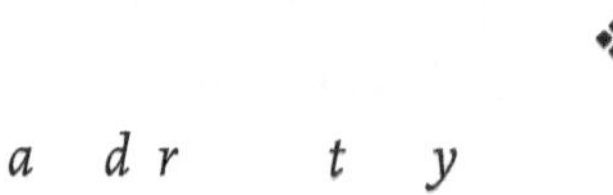

They were late on the day they moved in. I was handing over the keys in person for the cottage, because they came from so far away, you understand? Oh, it was convenient. Better than having them stay in a hotel overnight, and the moving van was coming early. 6am, I think. So I was stuck waiting, in the middle of that storm... Patricia, or whatever it was. Thunder so loud you could shout and not hear yourself, lightning illuminating the whole fen, all the lakes flaring white. Beautiful really, but torrential rain and no signal here for texts to reach me to say they were delayed, so not their fault. Couldn't be helped.

No, I didn't meet the twins then. Jay and Clara came in for the keys alone when they arrived. I didn't meet the twins until much later, a week or more perhaps. In the cafe it was. Well they seemed quiet, somewhat withdrawn, but that's hardly out of the ordinary considering what happened to them, what they went through... As for what happened, it's awful. Awful. Gut wrenching. I can't imagine how Jay and Clara must have felt, how they're feeling now. But yes, we all knew things weren't right. We could all see that family was falling apart. Those poor kids, and people didn't help. They gossip, don't they.

I hope some of those nosey old bints are suffering guilt. They ought to, god knows.

No, no. Look I know what was *said* about how those kids died, but it must have been out on the fens. I'm telling you. Well because, no one drowns in their bed, it's not possible, and it wasn't homicide, they ruled out any possibility and I believe the verdict. No reason not to. What am I saying? I'm saying that they were off wandering a good deal, sometimes too long. I saw that. I witnessed it. Gave Luke a lift home once, close to midnight. He was exhausted, miles from home. Soaking wet. You understand me?

What I think is... I think they were missing that night, when Jay and Clara got home. That Jay and Clara went looking for them and found them like that out on the fens. And I think they couldn't bear it. You understand?

They wanted them to be sleeping. Only sleeping.

❖

I   a   r   n

Laurel leans up to watch when they pass the line of wrecked cars, illuminated red by a succession of taillights. The front car is nothing but a black skeleton. Perhaps the engine exploded, the firemen driven back by roaring flames and flying metal. Bodies roasting. The road is wet, but there are puddles of darkness she imagines must be blood. They died hard, these people. How many? So many cars ruined, concertinaed behind the black skeleton of the first into a single entity. Vividly, she can imagine the bodies inside, woven together.

She lies back down and closes her eyes.

Water roars in her ears – the chaos and screams above mute and fly away, so very far. Part of her wants nothing more than to let go and sink deep. Deeper. Give in to the lull, the roaring in her ears. The weight of water. But when she opens her eyes for one last look, imagining the blue vault of it above flickering with the reflections of flames and sunlight, the water churns red, and there is a face floating in front of her. A face without a body, eyeless, the mouth a gaping window to red water.

It flies into her mouth when she screams, tangling around her tongue, warm and rubbery. Metallic.

This is not her first kiss.

Breathing in, she opens her eyes. Bites her lip until thin copper leaks onto her tongue. Watches police lights, blue and red, flashing in the drops on the window, melting and merging. Floats in the stillness, in the rain, in the quiet water of her body.

❖

Luke wakes choking, a familiar taste in his throat, thick and metallic. There's something stuck inside, filling his entire throat, impeding breath. Sour spit flooding his mouth, he lurches up, knocking the headboard against the wall. The lump shifts and he lets out a sound – rough panic. Curling over his tangled sheets, he gags, violent, his entire gut wrenching, acid rising hot and heavy to lap against the obstruction. He gags again, tearing up from the force of it, the burn of the acid, and the lump slides free, over his tongue, flops out onto the pale yellow of the candlewick spread.

A chunk of something, slick and purplish, stinking of water and rot. It soaks into the soft fabric, a spreading circle of brown liquid.

Rearing back, he smacks into the headboard, the back of his skull colliding with brick, roaring white noise into his ears, distant ringing pain. He hears screaming, muffled by water, the slap of bodies hitting the waves, the waves hitting the sides of the boat. His chest constricts, too tight. There's water pressing down, pressing in, and she's in his mouth again. She's always in his mouth. And on his sheets, her scrap still there, the circle of brown growing ever wider. Sobbing, he stuffs hands into his mouth, trying to drag the taste of her from his tongue. There's blood and acid. Salt and filthy water.

Meat and memory. Nothing more.

He wakes in buttery daylight, pain locked into his shoulders, the back of his neck. His head hurts, a slow, dull hurt like a headache. Wincing, he lifts a hand to rub it away, smelling spit and the sour edge of vomit on his skin. His gaze slides to the candlewick. The wide brown stain marring the soft yellow fabric, soaked through. Her remnant is gone, but it was there. It was there.

He can feel the shape of it lodged in his throat, slipping back down.

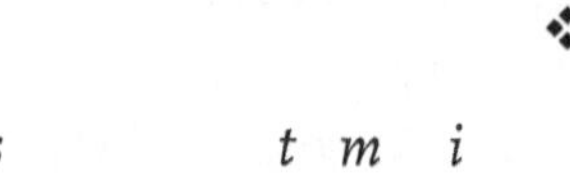

The fens are mostly drained, turned to arable land, but the land here remembers water in the same way her body does. It leaks out of the ground and surrounds her, mirror-smooth, mist rising from its surface like breath in cold air, rippling into strange reflections. Building pictures – worlds made of water. Ghosts in water vapour. People walking in lines, careful, across boggy land, leading cattle and children. Or cottages, smoke winding its way up into cloud, or drifting down in light wind to melt into the mist and be lost. Doorways. Worlds over the world.

On bad days, the mist writhes into bodies without faces, faces without bodies. Water follows her on those days, leaking out beneath her feet, leaching from the walls, from her skin. Leaving her smelling of copper and salt, that cool brackish scent of ocean mingled with blood. The mist rises from her skin then and forms eyeless masks, screaming mouths that open wide, wider, gaping to vast holes the wind howls through. Worlds and ghosts, all screaming at her.

❖

After. There's a word with new meaning. Loaded. It's like a line has been gouged, separating his life into two pieces, then and now. If he squints he imagines he can see it, an ugly black line, a barricade. But is he trapped inside or outside? He can't figure it out. The world feels distant and too close, too raw, too loud and full and suffocating, but he can't touch anything, or nothing touches him. Everything he feels is inside. Trapped. Waiting to come up. He may choke on it.

Lights out. The dark laps like water.

He sits, unable to sleep, shivering, his gut churning arounds lumps and scraps. In the dark, nothing is familiar, even his body is a stranger. He's floating too far away, needs to find something solid to stand on before he disappears completely. There's nothing beneath his feet but water, boiling red. He throws off the covers and goes to find Lau, his twin, who's always been that. Who must be, even now.

They've told him where she is, that she's doing well, but they tell his parents that he's doing well too.

It's like they don't even know what the words mean.

Her room, like his, is private, and she's awake. Of course she is. Sat staring at the television, the sound off, light and colours playing across her face, across the walls. She looks around when he closes the door and her expression, tight before, relaxes just a little.

"You're here," she says.

"Yeah."

"Watch with me."

He drags the big chair from the corner and they sit in silence, watching the show, a re-run of some old 80s sitcom. At some point he reaches out to take her hand and she clings to him like they're both still drowning. Or he clings to her. Perhaps they cling to each other, pretending that's what happened in the water, when neither of them really remember, not really. The only thing they know for sure, because they were told, is that they were far apart, that one of them almost wasn't found. They won't say which one.

Luke thinks it's both of them.

The sitcom finishes. There's a movie then, black and white. He watches without watching. All he notices is her hand in his, too warm, trembling. Halfway through, her grip tightens to the point of pain and she whispers:

"Don't ask. And don't tell me. We should never say. Swear to me."

He wakes in his own room, disorientated in the darkness, the quiet hum of the hospital at near rest. Did he find her? Was that real? It seems unlikely, not here, not with so many people watching them, so many worried eyes tracking their every move, every expression. But they must have found one another somehow, because no matter what else is gone, the promise remains, as clear as the line between before and after. Sworn.

We should never ask. Never tell. Swear to me.

❖

There was a storm on the day they arrived. Patricia. She escorted them in. Storm Edda is escorting them out in bursts of thunder and lashing rain.

Clara's not sad to go. This place has stolen from her. Everything. She could happily see it burn to ash, see it smashed to dust. They came here so hopeful, their children rescued from the water but still drowning. They believed this place might save them, instead it offered them to water – like sacrifices. How did she not see the water beneath the soil, waiting, predatory? Filling their footsteps until it became an ocean, vast and unfeeling. And so hungry.

She watches out the window, hating every inch of this place. Her heart clenches within her, an aching knot of muscle. It will never unfurl.

As they approach Ely, the cathedral rising through cloud like a judge, two hares, pure white, emerge from between the trees like darting lights, will-o'-the-wisps. They race the car for what seems like miles, appearing and vanishing, fleet of foot and fanciful. Edda grows fierce around them, pounding them with rain, with jagged forks of lightning clawing down from the heavens, lighting the clouds, those jagged billows, those hungry mouths, those weeping eyes. When their light fades, the hares have vanished. The storm has swallowed them whole.

Or perhaps they've fed themselves to it.

Faith Leaps

Kath Deakin & Tim Lebbon

On a dark and stormy night, the woman in red leather asked Leon if he wanted a jump.

She had piercings: a whole hanging-garden in her ears, a fine stud in her nose, left eyebrow pinched by a ring into a permanent quizzical arch. Her head was shaven, mapped with what appeared to be an intricate spider-web tattoo. But when Leon looked closer, and a new song blasted light from the reactive lighting rig, he realised that they were scars.

She came nearer. "A jump?"

Her eyes were a cross between green and gold, dazzling in this darkened room, picking up every scrap of light and reflecting it with an arrogant insistence that she be noticed. She was tall and trim and beautiful in the blood-red leather. She quite evidently did not know anyone else in the big house.

And Leon would have noticed her the moment he'd joined the party... had she been there first.

"Where did you come from?" he asked. He leant forward to do so, trying to defeat the guitars and drums pounding at the air, and he could smell her now as well. Oh yes, he would have noticed her.

The girl stared unflinchingly into his eyes. "Just dropped in."

Leon had been here for over two hours and although Nathan and the rest professed to being cool, interesting and decadent, they were really just a bunch of college graduates too comfortable with their successes to have any sense of rebellion in their lean, mean and fit to be seen bodies. They drank to excess (but only beers, no spirits), took drugs (marijuana, and then tempered by too much tobacco), listened to whatever the media prescribed at the time as evil or grotesque music (Marilyn Manson at the moment, Sex Pistols of the Nineties)... in short, they were boring. Pseudo-punks with the attitudes of slightly annoyed accountants. They would go far, Leon was sure, but in many ways, they were already as good as dead.

This girl though... she was beautiful and sad, staring at him with the haunted, fascinating expression of a war refugee. He knew that no one at the party could possibly know her, because she was for real.

"You don't even know me," Leon said, but the knowledge that she had picked him out from the rest gave him a thrill. She didn't know him, but she wanted to fuck.

The girl came even closer until he could smell her breath. It was stale and musky, as if she had not eaten or drunk for days. He realised how worn she actually looked. She reached out and touched his face, fingers tracing the scar from just below his mouth, over his chin and down to where it terminated at his Adam's apple. As she did so Leon looked closer at her head, at the network of scars crissing and crossing her scalp like an impossible jigsaw. She was a girl who had been lost, found and put back together. He wondered whether any parts were missing. This close, looking into her eyes, he realised the likelihood of that was great.

He had always found madness alluring.

"Sorry," the girl said, frowning. "I thought you were one of us."

"One of who?"

She shook her head and turned to leave. The pulsing coloured lights slid fluidly across her leather-clad body and she glanced back, once, just to confuse him more.

Leon reached out to clasp her shoulder but missed.

Nathan breathed smoke at him and shouted "Leon, you old fuck, we've got some splendid shit here!"

The girl nudged her way between cavorting bodies in the big dining room. If they noticed her, they decided not to show it.

He pushed after her, but for him the dancers were less yielding. Shoulders bumped, hands grasped, and all the while Red-Leather was moving further and further away. At last, in the hallway, he caught a glimpse of her disappearing around the curve in the staircase. He followed eagerly, tripping up the stairs.

Now this is more like it, he thought as he looked back through the dining room door at his so-called friends.

Along the tacky Egyptian-themed upstairs corridor a door clicked shut. Leon ran to it and opened it without knocking. The bathroom was empty. The window was wide open and the curtains swung back into position as he watched.

There was a sudden silence from downstairs as the music stopped. For a crazy moment Leon expected laughter, group-mockery at some weird joke played upon him by people who knew no better.

Then someone changed the CD, and the party dragged itself toward its own useless demise.

Charlie stared at the little crown of froth in the centre of her coffee cup, watching it turning round and round, echoing the motion of the teaspoon she'd just removed. If she concentrated hard enough, she found that she could blank out everything else: the steamed window pane a few feet in front of her; the subdued murmur from the rest of the café's customers; the winter sunlight flashing briefly on the heavy stream of cars in the street outside.

But she couldn't blank out who she was. She was Charlie, and she'd failed again.

A tiny droplet of moisture splashed into the teaspoon on the chequered tablecloth, and she realised she was crying again. "Oh no," she breathed to herself, "not now. Think of other things." But she could not. She looked up, and the miserable effort she'd made to appear competent and calm in the eyes of a potential employer stared mistily back at her from the windowpane. Too little experience, not the right experience, too much experience by far… it all amounted to the same thing in the end – unemployable. They would reel off the usual justifications, but Charlie was well aware that the reason they wouldn't employ her was because she couldn't meet their eyes, and she stammered and shook when anyone looked directly at her.

She stirred her coffee again and concentrated on the spinning, diminishing froth, trying once more to blank it all out.

Something made her glance up. Perhaps she'd sensed the face staring at her, not from outside but from within, a reflection watching her own as intently as she'd been staring into her coffee cup.

"You should try jumping," a voice said.

Charlie turned and looked at the thin young man sat in a wheelchair at the next table.

"I tried and couldn't do it... but you would," he said. "I'm sure."

His eyes were bright and blue and full of life and laughter, so friendly that she did not feel diminished beneath their gaze. There was a deep scar pulling down the corner of his left eyelid and trailing around his face to the hairline above his ear.

He reached over and placed a folded piece of paper in her hand. "I'll say no more," he said. "It's your choice entirely. As always." Then he smiled and wheeled himself out into the sunshine.

Charlie's 'flat'. She used the term loosely. It was in a building – it had walls, a roof, some furniture and even a sink – but otherwise it was a hole. There were roaches under the bed, the cistern leaked, damp was climbing the walls, the old wiring stank of potential fires and her fridge seemed designed specifically to rot food. Her childhood pet rabbit had enjoyed better living conditions that this.

She sat on the bed with her head in her hands, then pushed up her sleeves and stared at the punctured flesh they covered. She'd gazed at these scars every day since she'd 'woken up' – that first day when she'd been able to take in her surroundings without the image being filtered through her addiction. Everything was still more real than she could sometimes take. In moments like these she almost prayed for the chemical distance that blanked out the painfully obvious.

She wept yet again. This was her new life, the one promised by the counsellors and doctors. For the three months since she'd finally got clean, all she had known was disappointment, failure, form filling and the pain of having no buffer against being herself. She was clean, yes, but life hurt more than ever.

As the snot started to bubble and dribble from her nose she reached into her pocket for a tissue. Her hand came out holding the piece of paper, the one given to her by that strange guy in the café. She wiped her nose on her sleeve and read it:

> *"18 Tunnel Towers – midnight – rooftop.*
> *Unprecedented opportunity."*

Leon went for a walk.

He couldn't get the girl out of his mind. The previous night's party had drifted on with more shouting, more inane performances, and Leon had pushed through the sweating mass of bodies and left without any of them noticing. Around the back of the big house, below the bathroom window, a flowerbed lay unmolested, the roses colourless in the night. The window was still open, net curtain waving in the breeze like a reluctant goodbye.

No girl. No sign at all.

So he had gone home.

Now, tonight, he felt just as useless, directionless, futile, wasteful and wasting as he had last night. The only difference was that now he was all alone.

He walked a lot because there was little else for him to do. He had no money – the occasional jobs came and went, and he suited none of them – and what little he did receive in benefit went on rent for his one-room flat and what food he could then afford. He relied on others to provide distraction, feigning attachment to people he neither cared about nor understood. In return, he provided *them* with a project – help the helpless, ease his pain.

But walking was *his* thing. And it revealed an inherent masochism, because it allowed him to think.

As always when he walked – aimless and without intent, maybe, but still under leash to his past – he ended up there. There was no pavement, no path, no route marked for people to come and see. Simply an unremarkable grass verge... and a tree.

Leon had found himself here countless times since the crash, trying to deny his deeply embedded guilt, scoffing at the idea of responsibility even as he hugged the scarred wood and sank to his knees and cried. He would cry for a long time. It was not because he felt a sense of loss, but rather because he did not. He couldn't understand that. It didn't work.

Sometimes the sun would rise to find him wrapped around the tree, crying into glaring rush-hour headlights.

He ran his fingers across the wounded wood. The impact had shattered the bark and gouged into the healthy young trunk, just as his daughter's journey through the windscreen had cleaved her own flesh. Each time he came here he tried to imagine where her head had struck, knelt to trace the darker patches where he could touch her still.

He felt no guilt. Only hate. Hate at a God who could arbitrarily kill like this.

He had been angry. He had been shouting, ranting, raving, calling his girlfriend a bitch and bemoaning the fact that life was so unfair, why should he suffer, he had not been born to suffer with her and the kid sucking his life away... he had only taken his eyes from the road for a second, when she said that all his problems were his own fault... and maybe she'd been right... but he had not been to blame for the crash. When there was death, and a mourning so black and emotionless that he knew he could never find a way from its tarry depth, fault is too common a human failing to consider.

He had never wanted the child. He had never wanted this grief. What he really mourned was his own inadequacy.

And what made him cry was his inability to pass this point.

Something crunched beneath his knees. He reached down, already knowing what he found find, and pulled up a ragged bunch of rotted flowers, still wrapped in a torn plastic cover.

She had been here again.

"There's always hope, you know."

He let out a grunt and spun around, overbalancing and falling with his back to the tree, his foot twisted beneath him. Red-Leather stood before him, dressed almost as she had been the night before but with a heavy jacket bulking her out.

"You," he whispered. "Where did you go?"

She ignored his question. "Hope is never eternal, but it can spring from the strangest of places. There are different types of hope, too. People like you will long to know everything at the point of death, because you'll have no use for it any other time. You'll hope that experience and hate and apathy can combine to give you total knowledge at the moment you slip away, the final dreadful irony. Know everything and have nothing to do with it. Too late."

She was silent for a moment, staring past or through him at the tree, and further even than that. A passing car's headlights caught her eyes and they were open wide.

"I only hope that I can avoid who I am, just for a moment," Leon whispered.

Again, she ignored him. "Another type of hope is the passive one. I used to be like that. I used to wish..." She scratched her arm at the elbow, breathed a shaking sigh. "I used to wish my life would just sort itself out. But I was too wasted to help it."

"Why are you following me?"

She stared at him. It was dark, the only light coming from the almost-full moon, and he could not see her eyes. But he could feel her stare.

"Others take matters into their own hands," she said quietly. "You can hope all you want... but you know what they say: you can't hope yourself right, but you can *help* yourself."

"I thought it was 'The Lord helps those who help themselves'?"

She shrugged. "Whatever."

"Well forget it. I don't care."

They were silent for a while. Leon stood shakily and leant back against the tree, glancing over Red-Leather's shoulder at the road along which he had travelled, once in a car, a hundred times since on foot.

"You can jump," she said. "Tonight. I'll show you. It'll hurt. It always does the first time – if you hit bottom, anyway – and you'll be left with the mark. But then you'll know."

"Know what?"

"What it is not to hate yourself."

Leon snorted. "Bullshit. Jump where? Jump what? You?"

"I've jumped, yes. Many times."

"*Fuck* you?" A statement or a question, even Leon could not decide for sure.

Red-Leather shook her head. "Jump *with* me, I mean," she said. "Look, you've got the choice and the chance. I can do no more than that. Not as if I can pick you up and throw you."

She turned and walked away.

"Wait!" Leon shouted.

"Come with me," she said, without looking over her shoulder.

"Where to? Why?" But Red-Leather was disappearing into the night, a shadow merging with other shadows until all grew still once more. Did she really expect him to follow some crazy woman into the dark, a mad woman talking like a Noughties Jesus on crack?

He closed his eyes...

...his girlfriend screamed at him, he raged back, banging his fist on the dashboard so that he did not bring it down on her, Anne cried in the back seat because Mummy and Daddy were arguing, the engine raced, the steering became liquid, the impact, the warm wet spray of blood from his throat, the cooler sense of someone else's splashing him, more screaming... more, more screaming...

His eyes snapped open. He strode away from the tree in the footsteps of Red-Leather, trying to convince himself even now that he was only walking back into town, not following her at all, not thinking about what she had said.

Fooling himself as ever, Leon took the first step towards the greatest leap of his life.

Clouds smothered the moon. And although it was still early in September the cold bit hard, and Charlie's breath plumed in the faint light from the street below. She began to wish she'd worn more, and then laughed quietly. She didn't *have* more.

Why she was here was still completely unfathomable to her. What could she gain from sitting on a dark rooftop on a cold autumn night? The view? It *was* good, that much had already penetrated her misery. The sounds of the city were filtered and distant and, from here, the lights and buildings spread out below were imbued with a beauty that was entirely absent whilst living amongst them. She leaned against the rusty railing that topped the roof parapet. *Otherworldly...* the word appeared in her head as she picked out her own street. She turned to the doorway to go back down to street level. Her breath stuck in her throat.

A crowd had gathered.

She stood still, staring at the figures moving indistinctly in the rooftop gloom. Each pair of eyes shone brightly back at her, picking up and magnifying the gentle cityscape luminosity. They stood there in silence, no one betraying the slightest surprise that she should be up on this rooftop in the middle of the night. A shadow separated from the crowd and moved towards her. She cowered back against the railing as the figure approached, unable to comprehend the two pairs of eyes moving independently of one another.

"Can you feel it?"

It was the voice of the wheelchair-bound man from the café. Charlie blinked her incomprehension and fear at the shape. It moved closer to the railing and into the glow from the streetlights below, separating into her mysterious messenger from the café and a strongly built middle-aged man, carrying the thin man on his back. They disengaged, leaving the thin man sat on the wall beside her while his ride moved back to merge once again with the gloom.

"Turn around," he told her. "Just look at it."

"What do you want?" she whispered.

"Nothing. But you want... you lack... well, I could tell," he whispered.

"What are you offering me?" Charlie replied, louder. "I know I look ... I behave like I need something, but I'm clean." She shook her head, lied. "I don't want it anymore."

"You'll find all that's irrelevant." He leaned closer to her. "There's no harm here. Just these people and me. We've done this before, believe me... there's no harm. Just turn around and look at the lights."

Compelled to do as he asked, she stared out across the city spread below her.

As she looked her eyes lost their focus, and the view became a glorious amalgam of colours that made it someplace else. She could smell the hint of fresh air in the smog of traffic fumes cooling her cheeks, she could hear the distant cacophony of night-time voices, music, traffic and sirens blending into an unreal symphony. As her focus blurred even more, she felt herself detach from her surroundings. She could no longer feel the rough corroded railing in her grip or the discomfort from her tight-fitting boots. She was in amongst the lights, a thousand miles from this rooftop, from *any* rooftop...

A flashing sense of vertigo hit her, followed immediately by an acute and breath-taking fear. The railing became solid in her grasp once more. She started breathing heavily, blinking to clear her eyes. There were shapes moving in the street below her. She turned around and saw that she was alone.

Or almost alone. The thin man was about to pass

through the door to the stairwell perched on someone else's back. He smiled at her. She was sure of this, even though light barely touched him. She could hear it in his voice.

"Someone always comes back to carry me down." As the door drifted shut on them, Charlie was sure she saw him wink. "Almost, eh?" And then she truly was alone.

She pulled herself up to sit on the wall. Eyes shut and head in hands, she felt painlessly hungover and incapable of thought. She opened her eyes and looked up as she heard the door opening once again. Another figure joined her on the rooftop.

"Hello, is that you?" a man's voice asked. His shadow walked rapidly towards her at the roof's edge. "I had to follow you..." He stopped with a gasp when he finally made out her face.

"Fucking hell... no!" He shook his head. "Charlie, what are you doing here?"

For the hundredth time that evening Charlie was lost for words. His was a face she hadn't seen for a long time, but here she was now, face to face with Leon, the putrid shit-fuck who'd broken her life apart.

He leaned against the wall beside her, staring out over the city below, apparently as lost for words as she. She glanced at his face and closed her eyes with a shudder. She hadn't seen him for four years and the scar running from his under his chin, though still pronounced, had faded. She took this in with one half of her mind. The other half was recoiling at the memory of her baby's shredded features, an image synonymous in her mind with the memory of this man's face, this bastard's fucking face. It had been her nightmare for four years, and the root of her addiction. A string of events on constant replay, in slow motion, again and again and again.

She gasped with the pain of it.

"I don't understand any of this," she heard Leon mutter, more to himself than to her.

"What are you doing here?" She could feel the venom rising with the bile his presence had provoked. She didn't wait for an answer. "Fuck off and leave me alone!"

"Not *my* doing," he responded. "Believe me, I don't need to see you either. I came for that woman. Is she here?"

It was as if the four years hadn't happened. She had been dismissed and sidelined already, secondary to his overwhelming urge to please himself. He leaned over the railing to get a better view of the street below. Charlie closed her eyes, and in her mind she rehearsed the push that would heal her pain.

"You looking for me?"

Charlie jumped and her eyes shot open. Leon turned towards the new voice.

A woman was approaching them from the rooftop door, the leather covering her body gleaming softly in the sodium-infused light. She stood between Charlie and Leon at the roof edge.

"I know what you're thinking, girl," she said, ignoring Leon. She leaned towards Charlie, bringing her mouth close to her ear. "Close your eyes," she whispered. Charlie breathed in the ozone smell of the woman's breath and did as instructed without thinking.

Eyes closed, impossibly, she watched Leon flailing his arms, windmilling as he fell back from the railing. She saw his look of sheer terror grow smaller and smaller as he plummeted towards the street, his mouth slowly shaping itself around a single word... *No...*

But now she was lying on the pavement below, looking up, watching Leon's shape shortening and elongating, painfully slowly, as he turned end over end over end...

He hit the ground beside her. She saw the bones in his body slowly detach from each other, connected only by the elasticity of his skin as he flattened out on the concrete. The pressure of disconnection becoming unbearable, his skin slowly came apart and spilled its contents across the pavement. His eyes, still wide open, stared into hers as their sockets crushed and distorted, piercing their soft jelly...

The scream welling in her chest finally broke free. She opened her eyes, afraid that she would see the same view but too terrified not to try. Leon was leaning against the wall, staring at her. She turned and saw that the girl in leather was also watching her, a wry grin creasing one corner of her mouth.

"Feel better now?" the girl asked.

Charlie's tentative hold on her nerve and her stomach-contents snapped. Desperate to be off the rooftop, she ran retching for the door, leaving Leon alone with his Red-Leather girl. She opened the door, sure she could hear laughter behind her but equally certain that it was her own inadequacy telling her that. She stopped on the landing and puked. The vomit pooled before her and dribbled down the metal-grilled staircase, filling the stairwell with an acidic stench.

She hated to puke. She seemed to have spent the last four years being sick.

If only she could expel her hatred for that bastard so easily.

"Girlfriend?" Red-Leather asked.

Leon shook his head. He could not take his eyes from her. Charlie had been and gone, and her brief presence had left nothing more than a sick feeling in his stomach, a sense of movement halted unnaturally... as if by a tree. This girl commanded his attention now. Even before he heard the rooftop door bang shut behind Charlie, he had forgotten her once more.

"She seemed eager to leave."

"Doesn't like me."

Red-Leather raised her eyebrows. "Stands to reason. You're not very likeable, are you?"

Leon looked down at his feet, the roof chippings scattered around his shoes like repulsed iron filings. "What am I doing here?" he asked, unsure whether the question was directed at himself or Red-Leather.

"Do you trust me?" she asked.

"I don't trust anyone."

"*Can* you trust me?" Her voice had changed, suddenly and without any break in what she was saying. It was as if they no longer stood on a cold, breezy roof in the middle of the night, but somewhere without echoes, no corners or walls or floor for her words to bounce back from, a place where words could go on forever. And instantly he knew that he *could* trust her, because there was no one else worth trusting. Charlie? She wanted him dead. Himself? He could rely on himself to bring pain and destruction, but that was all.

"Trust me?" Red-Leather said again, her voice so close now, close enough to be coming from inside his head, not without. She stood before him and her lips moved, but it was as if he knew what she was going to say and heard the words moments before they were uttered.

"You're distracting me," he said. "Since I first saw you last night, you've distracted me. I can't think of anything else." *Distracting me from my own pain and uselessness...*

"Trust me because I can help you," she cooed, ignoring what he had said.

He shook his head, but gently, because he did not want to dislodge the feeling settling in there. It was better than booze, better than drugs. "You're making me feel like someone else..."

"Deep inside, you are. Listen." He felt her hands on his shoulders and smelled her breath as she spoke, a curiously alien smell, a blown fuse combined with fresh roses. "You have to let go of your senses when you jump so that awareness doesn't hurt you. Sight, sound, touch, smell, taste... become neutral, nothing, and all possibilities are attainable." The smell of her breath faded to nothing. The feel of her hands on his shoulders lifted away. And then the sense of his shoulders actually being there at all left him.

"You... distract me," he said. "I feel like—"

"You're falling somewhere new," she said, though he hardly heard her.

And then the world tilted around them as she eased them both over the parapet and out into space.

Leon kept his eyes open, but he could not see. He opened his mouth to scream but could utter no sound. His tongue was dry, his mouth tasteless. He knew he was falling, although there was no sense of it – no wind rushing past his skin or whistling in his ears; no pull and tug as gravity hauled at his guts; no strain as acceleration pushed his brain against the inside of his skull.

And then, in his mind's eye, he saw the ground rushing up to meet him. Except it wasn't the ground. It was a tree, trunk so wide that he could never avoid it, so solid that he would spread across it, opening up for the night air to take its pick.

Strangely, he had no fear.

When he hit, all remaining senses fled, and the darkness that came in was absolute.

He opened his eyes.

"Leon?"

He was lying on his side. There was a pair of feet next to him, someone standing, someone clad in red.

"Leon?"

Oh God, he hurt. Every bone broken, surely, every organ bruised or worse. He must be breathing blood, bubbling it from his mouth, he could feel it leaking from a dozen rents in his flesh, spreading across the dark concrete, taking his mashed insides with it.

"Leon? How do you feel?" Red-Leather knelt by his side and gently lifted his head.

He groaned. "We fell."

She smiled. "It was a good one. It's been a few weeks for me, and it was a good one. Not quite perfect... but then I've yet to find perfect. But *you*... how do *you* feel?

"Ambulance," he gasped.

She shook her head, smiling. Weak starlight caught the jewellery in her ears and face, falling on him, daring him to catch it. "You don't need an ambulance."

And that was when most of the pain vanished. He sat up suddenly, amazed that he could move. "What have you done to me?"

"Helped you take a leap of faith."

"You're mad," he said, looking up, unable to see the rooftop from here because it was hidden in the night sky. "You threw me from the roof!"

"We jumped—"

"Threw me! Mad! Fucking *mad!*" He stood and ran. There was pain but he revelled in it, wishing it into his muscles and his bones and his brain. He did not hear her footsteps, but her voice followed him into the dark.

"Don't let it damage you, Leon, let it help you! Come back when you're ready. Next time you try it on your own!"

He shook his head, ran, ran.

Those scars on her scalp. He could see only those scars.

He realised that he was bleeding from a deep gash across his forehead. He didn't care. Good. Less blood inside, less of him to bleed away. Easier to finally die.

❖

Charlie had slept for hours, something she couldn't remember doing since Anne had been killed. She usually woke every hour to hear her daughter crying for her, and she had long given up trying to overcome her loss because she knew she never would. The reason she'd slept so well... she'd finally realised that she did not *have* to overcome her loss.

She had to live with it.

She had taken her usual seat in the café facing the window and sat drinking scorching coffee, waiting for her eggs and bacon. She was still smiling at her own reflection when her mysterious wheelchair-bound friend joined her. He tucked his wheels under the table just as her meal arrived.

"Excuse me," she said, "but I'm starving."

"Carry on," he replied, smiling. He watched in silence as she polished off her plateful of food. She ate noisily, having to wipe constantly at her lips and chin where fat dribbled, but relishing every single mouthful.

"Enjoy that?" he asked as she mopped up the remains of the egg yolk with some bread.

"Oh yes," she said, and flashed him a smile. She liked his eyes.

She finished her coffee and they sat in silence, staring at each other's reflections in the window.

"I haven't a clue what's going on," she said, "but that's the first time I've *really* tasted food in four years."

"Really?"

"I feel very awake." She giggled. "You know, I watched the man I blame for my life of shit die horribly last night in front of my eyes."

"You did?" he asked, perhaps not as surprised as he should have been.

"And now I realise what a pointless exercise this blame thing is. In my mind he was dead. I really believed what I was seeing. And you know what?"

"What?"

"It made absolutely no difference to me whether he was dead or alive. I'd still lived the same four years. Of course, if he'd never been born that would be a different story."

They stared at each other, Charlie feeling unreasonably comfortable meeting this stranger's gaze.

"So if it made no difference, why so cheerful?"

"I enjoyed watching him die."

"Oh?"

"And I realised that I didn't hate him because of what happened."

"Right."

"He's always been a stupid irresponsible self-obsessed fuck, and I know now I hated him from the first day I saw him. Ultimately, his shittiness is his problem. It's just taken me this long to see that."

The thin man stared at her in what she thought was complete dumbstruck astonishment. Then he fell forward in his chair, put his head on the table and started emitting an awful choking sound. It was only when he lifted his head and wiped his eyes that she understood he was laughing.

"That's just great!" he gasped. "Great!"

"So, 'Rolly'," she said to more choking laughter, "what's next?"

❖

Alone in his flat, Leon sat and tried to understand what had happened.

Blood caked his forehead and face. The cut needed stitches, though as he thought about that he seemed to hear Red-Leather's voice in his mind: *don't do that, it scars better without.* But it was not the woman's imagined voice, nor fear, nor exhaustion that kept him where he was, sitting staring at a blank wall and seeing... what? What had happened? *That's* what occupied him now. The truth, about something that was impossible.

He had fallen from the roof. More accurately, he'd been pushed – or pulled – over by Red-Leather. Had she fallen with him? Surely she had. He'd tumbled over the parapet with her...

And yet at the bottom, six floors down, she was standing next to him when he came around. Waiting to talk. As if nothing bad had happened.

Six floors.

He should be dead.

He sighed, leaned forward and cradled his head in his hands. He'd been offered a glimpse of something today, he was sure, something rare and exquisite and precious, but just as he'd let his own daughter slip through his fingers, so he was doing the same with this. He tried to think of Anne playing on the floor, rolling around on their bed, building unknown baby-sculptures with blocks and giggling at her own imagination. But the only picture he could conjure was of her rag-doll flight over his shoulder and into the windscreen... and through... and after...

Nothing else would come, so he went outside onto his floor's landing, opened the window and stared out. Three floors down, straight onto glass-strewn concrete, a pavement littered with used condoms and junkies' needles, some of the needles his own. He needed a fix.

Better than any fix, a voice said in his head, but he did not recognise it so it only served to scare him more.

Three floors. Two seconds, perhaps, during which time he would either come to realise some amazing truth about Red-Leather and all she had said, or his pathetic life would flash before him in preparation for a broken-boned death. Red-Leather seemed so genuine, so frank, so beautiful in her battered self-regard.

This is what you need, that voice said again. Leon spun around, ready to fight whoever was standing behind him taunting and cajoling. Red-Leather come to help him out, perhaps. But there was no one there.

He closed his eyes and tried to remember what he'd felt during his six floor fall, but there was nothing. Only that voice once more, telling him how good it could be, how much he would take control of his life by shunning the drugs and the hate and the apathy to take the plunge into a new, brighter world.

And then he recognised the voice as his own.

Leon opened his eyes and shut the window. The whole fucking world was conspiring to drive him mad.

He went back into his flat to shoot up.

She had no more questions, no more doubts. It felt as natural as walking down a street.

Another dark rooftop, another panoramic city view.

Charlie knew that another silent crowd was gathering behind her. She could feel the change in atmosphere, the charge in the air, as if the mother of all storms was about to manifest right there over the rooftop.

For some reason Leon's crushed and shattered image, constant in her head since the previous night, had been replaced with a picture of her daughter. Not in the aftermath of the crash, but whole and healthy and laughing and loving. She hadn't pictured Anne this way for four years. The few photographs Charlie possessed always failed to bring Anne back to life, but now there she was, living again just for her.

Tuning into her surroundings once more, she found that she had climbed the parapet and stood with her ankles leaning against the low railing. Up here, she was more exposed to the fresh breeze blowing an autumn chill through the city. Looking down at the streets, watching cars finding their way uncertainly through the warren of streets and late-night crowds, she felt utterly disconnected. It was another world. *This* was where she should be, elevated above everything.

She glanced to her side as one by one her rooftop companions took their places along the parapet. Their faces, some bearing obvious scars, all shared the same expression of total serenity. She closed her eyes and felt the wind grow stronger, but there was no chill to it now, and she could no longer feel the pressure of the railing against her ankles, and her weight had lifted from her heels.

The images that had haunted her over the years

vanished as if she'd opened her brain to a vacuum. The wind blew through her head as it stroked through her hair.

Breathing deeply, she opened her eyes.

She was in amongst the lights, a part of them. She was spread across the city. She encompassed all she could see. It was so vast. And she was just a particle. One of a thousand pinpoints of light.

She was falling. She could feel it. At what seemed an unimaginable speed. She was falling, but nothing grew any closer.

The fall was endless.

Charlie gave herself a final check over in the mirror and nodded approval at what she saw. One of her greatest pleasures now was being able to wear short sleeves in this warm weather. She looked more closely at her arms, still amazed at how well the track marks had cleared. There were no scars.

There was plenty of time before she was due at work, but she planned to walk this morning to take advantage of the sun. As she opened the front door of the townhouse she shared with her new boyfriend, her neighbour passed by, shepherding two young children along the street to school. Charlie called a 'good morning' after her and watched them on their way, the two girls' shining curls bouncing as they ran.

She smiled contentedly and rested her hands on her swollen stomach. "Not much longer," she whispered to her unborn child. Then she stepped out into the sunlight.

❖

He knew that she'd walked into the café when the conversation dipped slightly behind him.

She took hold of his wheelchair and manoeuvred it so that she could sit comfortably by his table. She was wearing her familiar red leather, even in this heat.

She unfolded the newspaper and placed it on the table in front of him.

"I honestly didn't expect there to be a fuss," he said. "She was so *alone*, for fuck's sake."

"Not quite, eh?" Red-Leather replied with a sardonic grin.

He read the headline: 'Local Woman's Disappearance Still a Mystery'. The photograph of Charlie stared back at him, a drab passport-style snap at least four years old. Underneath was a photo of her parents at the press conference, tearfully appealing for news of her whereabouts. She'd been so utterly, totally alone... he couldn't understand how these seemingly devoted parents could have allowed her to live like that.

"Perhaps they'd already done everything they could," Red-Leather said, reading his mind. "They'd probably already seen her disappear."

"She needed us, yes?" He stared at her seeking reassurance. "It was right?"

"Oh yes," she nodded emphatically. "*She* did. Leon... well, some people can never help themselves. Misery suited him."

He smiled. "She didn't hit bottom."

"No."

He nodded and stared down at the table in awe. "I wonder where they go."

She reached across and took hold of his hand. "I'm sure we'll find out." She touched his chin and lifted his face until he was looking at her. "We'll fall together someday. And we won't hit here."

Whispers After Dark
G.V. Anderson

Dark and stormy nights work best for wrecking, my Granfer always said. Excise men prefer to stay inside with a nip of brandy when it comes down hard – fat cats lazing by the Customs House fire, the lot of them – so we could stand safe on the cliffs west of Polperro as long as we liked. That's one of my earliest memories. Eight years old and wet through, shivering miserably for hours in the dark cos we carried no lights to give us away. Gorse snagging my breeches. I kept my eyes closed against the rain most of the night. I don't think I even stirred when the shout went up: a ship's light too close to shore. Like a stray star far from home.

Granfer got me moving with a cuff round the ear. I followed the men carefully along the cliff, my finger hooked into Granfer's coat pocket so I wouldn't get lost. There were four or five of us, the men rough. They smelled musky and sour. Coarse bristle covered their chins. The rain cut lines down their dirty faces, black from the mines. I was awed by them – them and my Granfer – and more than a bit scared of their fists.

Slowly, slowly, mud sucking at our ankles, we picked our way down to the beach. There be hundreds of them along the coast. Some of them hardly be beaches at all, but sheets of stone cut into ripples by the sea. This one, our one, was a shingle, set deep within the granite cliff. Hard to spot. I hated it – the jagged stones and shell shards always stabbed through the thin soles of my shoes.

The squall had blown itself out by the time the sky paled. Numb and salt-scabbed, we were the first down by the water that morning. Wrecking works like that, see: we're scavengers. Smuggling's different, dangerous. Smuggling's what the excise men will hang us for, unless we bribe them first. But picking up what's washed ashore after a ship's hit the rocks is our right, so long as there's no crew left alive to claim it.

Well, there was someone, that day. We didn't see him at first.

Casks of brandy lay smashed upon waterside. Gulls squabbled over what liquor lingered in the kegs' open bellies before the men chased them off. Bolts of sea-spoiled silk and green baccy clogged the rock pools. My Granfer and his men saved what they could, pulling things further up the beach to dry out, but it was a small pile: most of it had been lost to sea or washed up elsewhere. The men shouted at me to look for more so I skirted the swells, licking brine from my lips, until I reached the far end of the beach. With a hiss and clatter, the water broke, dragging flotsam with it. I kicked a broken cask. A surge obligingly swept it away.

I crouched there, hugging myself, but it didn't stop the ache in my belly.

Life was hard back then. Folk paid heavy taxes for the war with France and the price of grain was beyond the means of most, especially when the copper seams ran out and left the men with no wages. A side venture of liquor and baccy put coin in everyone's pocket, but lean salvage makes for a leaner month. At eight years old, I was just starting to learn that lesson. My guts were eating me inside-out, I was so hungry.

Aye, life was hard back then, but when's it not?

It's cos I'd hunkered low that I saw him. The sea had set him down past the craggy rocks that cut our beach off from another, smaller bank. His bare, bruised feet stuck out into the water.

No-one minded me. I clambered over the rocks to peer at him, hoping he'd be a Navy man, maybe an officer, like Father. Better yet, a captain! My tiny mind spun with excitement. But the man didn't have no blue coat with shiny buttons. He looked poorer than I – no, worse: Mama worked hard to keep me presentable. The man's waistcoat was gone, his breeches stiff with salt. His ankles were skinny, the tendon running down to his heel sharp as a blade.

"Hullo," I said, suddenly timid.

He heard me. Raised his pallid cheek. Mouthed something. *Water.*

"Colan!" my Granfer bellowed. I flinched. Nearly fell off the rock. "What 'ee got over there?" He was already on his way, huffing and crunching over the shingle.

I waved my arms. Grinned stupidly. "I found someone!"

I didn't understand the fear in my Granfer's face at first, nor the despair in his voice as he called to the others. They were thinking with their empty bellies and the cries of their children, the pittance we'd managed to collect so far. At any moment, rivals from the east could swoop in and leave us with even less. And now this man, low as he looked, with his right to every bit of salvage... Perhaps this was kinder; yes, kinder. Or at least less cruel. He'd only have died alone on the beach otherwise, drowning when the tide came in.

Granfer pushed me out the way. Without stopping for his men – not needing to know what they'd say – he climbed over the rocks, fished about for a sharp piece of slate, yanked the man's head back by his ratty hair, and slashed his neck. Then he parked one fist on his hip and waited for the dark, thick spurts of blood to stop.

He'd made more fuss butchering pigs.

Granfer sold the plunder for a paltry profit. Mama made it stretch, somehow. She paid our rent, settled unseen debts, such things that hardly matter to an eight-year-old. I wonder if she knew what we'd done for that money. What it cost us. I don't like to think of her turning a blind eye to murder, but then she *was* Granfer's daughter.

That streak runs through me too, lurid as a copper seam. Never constant, though; not like Granfer's. I'm sure he lost no sleep over it, but I've lain awake for many nights thinking of the Navy man's neck and the hollow whistle of his breath escaping when the blood finally had done. We couldn't risk leaving his body for someone to find. The men wrapped him up in sailcloth and dropped him off the cliff. He never came back to our beach. The current must've took him away.

Still, that whistle.

Granfer ran goods from time to time. A proper smuggler then, he was. When I got older, before I got too old to spend half my life down the mines, I helped carry the loot through tunnels in the cliff, or else watched for the excise men's red coats while others unloaded the boats. A whistle was how we smugglers worked in the dark. It meant *swag*, or *move it*, or *watch out!* How many times have I stood waiting upon beach, my bones grating with cold – or sat lately by the kitchen fire – listening out for a friendly whistle and hearing instead the wheeze of a ruined throat?

"Don't 'ee tell a soul, boy," Granfer said to me once the Navy man's body stopped twitching. It were a hazy dawn – sunlight everywhere and nowhere, catching in the net of Granfer's thinning hair. When I couldn't look at him, he pinned my shoulder against the rocks with the heel of his hand, the bloody slate still pinched between his fingers. "Breathe a word of this and I'll make 'ee sorry, long as I live." I believed him. A life down the mines had given him a mean hunch to his back, like he was curling up on himself. Storing his strength. I'd seen him swing at people in anger. Mama always fixed his knuckles afterwards. If he took a swing at me, would she fix his knuckles first, or my face? So, I stayed quiet. I let that deathly whistle claw at me for years, even as we kept watching for wrecks. No-one else washed ashore, but the ships that broke apart on the rocks still spilled lives into the sea along with their booty. Up on the cliff, we whooped and cheered our good fortune.

❖

Granfer often joked it would be the gibbet for him. It squeals at the slightest breeze, this thing, rusted the colour of red sandstone. The cage dangles freely over Talland Bay. They say it's the best view in Cornwall. Anyway, Granfer never got the pleasure cos he went in his own bed as quietly as you please, and Mama had him buried in the churchyard like a proper gentleman.

I was head of a household at sixteen.

At the funeral, Mama saw the worry on my face. She cupped and kissed it sadly. The fuzz around my jaw was darkening, but it was a child's face still. It must have pained her, to see there the concern that should have been Father's. But he was at sea – always at sea, no matter how many times I asked, no matter that other Navy men got shore leave or sent money home. We never got visits, nor any such money. Not even a letter. Eventually, I came to understand that 'at sea' was just something Mama put about so no-one asked difficult questions.

We were alone, then. The adult world was opened to me at last: we were and had only ever been one tenuous cycle of credit and payment away from the workhouse. Mama had borrowed money to bury Granfer properly and my wages from the mines barely covered the interest. We lived week to week, just the two of us. A humble living. Thankfully neither of us needed much.

Things changed when I married Eseld, who soon started popping out babies. The look on Mama's tired face when I placed Jowanet, our daughter, in her arms was worth the worry of an extra mouth to feed, though she missed the chance to meet her grandson, Ruan.

When our third came along, Bryon, and quickly died, we cried with relief and hated ourselves for it. The war was done by then but the price of grain hadn't recovered, and copper seams all over the coast were petering out, or else they glimmered beyond reach in flooded chambers no pump could drain; I had little work. Jowanet and Ruan were already such skinny things, shorter than other children. Poor Bryon would've starved if he'd lived. Perhaps it went kinder on him to leave hardly before he began; yes, kinder. Or at least less cruel.

I started wrecking again with a new crowd, running goods. The excise men had changed since I was a boy — they still served themselves, of course, but the reward for an arrest far outstripped a smuggler's bribe – and the iron gibbet saw heavier use. An old friend of Granfer's, one of the men who'd scared me so, rotted there even as we headed down to the beach one morning. We could hear the gulls shrieking as they pecked out his eyes.

A ship had gone down in the night. I'd seen it the day before, sitting low and laden in the water. Lately arrived from Portugal, it had been blown off course by a vicious gale, and then bested by our choppy waters. The wind whistled in the narrow chines down to the shore; it pushed urgently at my back. Upon beach, we found treasure like I never seen before. Whole boxes of saffron, dry and perfect. Thick, fragrant clumps of baccy wrapped in oilcloth. Barrels and barrels of Portuguese wine.

We found survivors, too. Slaves still in irons, half-drowned, and seamen staggering to their feet. Two were officers. The sea air had scoured the colour from their coats, but their cuffs still shone blue.

The men I ran with looked to me, made a leader of me where we'd had none. Their heads turned but their eyes came last, reluctant to let the goods out of sight.

"What do we do, Colan?"

My Granfer would've bled the survivors dry by now, that lurid streak showing itself. I said to them, "What say you all? Quick now, before they get their bearings," and as soon as the words left my mouth, I knew I was no more than asking permission. I'd already made up my mind to strike first. I saw a year of good meals for my family in the saffron alone. Our rent paid, our debts cleared, maybe even a little put aside; such things that matter a great deal when you're grown. My men felt the same. But this wasn't like Granfer putting some poor soul out of its misery. This was bloody, tight-lipped murder. We were matched in numbers and strength, just, so it came down to our nerve. God forgive us, we didn't even break the slaves' irons first to give them a fighting chance.

One, I throttled. The ship's boy, I think, scrawny enough for a single hand to encircle his neck. How easy it is, and yet how hard, to crush a windpipe. How long you must cling to your sin, to be sure it's done, till the lips of the dead turn quite blue.

Eseld comes from the moor where the granite backbone of Cornwall breaches the land like a whale's back. She's not coastal folk like me. Smuggling's not in her blood, nor that copper streak. Whenever the whistle came of a night – *a new shipment's come* – she'd narrow her eyes and ask me exactly where I thought I was going.

My cut of the saffron bought her a new dress. A peace offering. She refused to wear it. I wouldn't tell her how I came to pay for it, but she knew it had something to do with my lying awake in the bed beside her, rubbing at my hands. If they fell still, the crunch of that boy's throat would tingle through the pads of my fingers. I'd started to hear whistling outside our window at odd hours. I'd spring out of bed and downstairs, only to open the door and find... nothing. Nothing and something. A weight. A shadow. A judgement.

"Did something go wrong with the last run?" Eseld asked. She chose her moment: our legs tangled, my hands scrunched in her hair. Content, dozy after such tender coupling.

"What makes you think that?"

She yawned, draped an arm across my chest with a careful, measured ease. "You're restless. And the dress—"

My heart was hammering. Could she feel it? I rolled up and over her, buried my face into her breasts. "Won't you wear it for me?"

She prised me off. Held me by the throat at arm's length. I had always liked that, before. "If you'll tell me what it cost."

"Let go."

"Tell me what you did."

"I said, *let go*."

Her eyes glinted strangely silver in the dark. A seam of tin, not copper. She opened her fingers and sat up with me, waiting for me to speak, and speak I did. Granfer was ash and sod: he couldn't frighten me anymore. I told her about the Navy man he'd killed. I then told her, more slowly, of the men we'd drowned and the boy I'd strangled with my own bare hands. Talking about it was like telling the story of someone else's crimes: I knew I'd done it – I could still feel the ghost of the boy's grip on my forearm, days later – but somehow, I'd tricked myself into thinking I hadn't been there at all.

And now, the whistles after dark. The heaviness outside our home. I sobbed, scared out of my wits. Everything had been for the benefit of Eseld, Jowanet and Ruan. Their comfort. I'd brought the Devil upon them instead.

"You trying to make a widow of me, you damned fool?" Eseld hissed, covering my mouth to muffle my cries. "These dead men will come looking for 'ee, sooner or later. Confess to them. Perhaps they'll take pity on 'ee." She glanced at the dress, slung over the back of a chair. "Burn that thing. It was folly to buy it."

She was right. I be the only son of a penniless spinster – widow, if people are being generous about Mama; whore, if they aren't – and grandson of a known rum-runner. I never ate three square meals in my life and, like a lot of folk, I often fall behind on my rent. When I purchased a new dress outright for my wife, revealing sudden, hitherto-unseen riches, the news spread fast.

Every morning, I held my children tight until they wriggled shyly away. Let them have cores of rare tin, clean as pearls like Eseld. God bless her. She stained her hands red helping me move the last of the saffron. It weren't enough. Her dress still smouldered in the hearth, refusing to burn, when the excise men came for me.

❖

They call it a hanging in chains, but there's no chains. Just iron bars. Below lie rocks rimmed with white sea-foam, and ahead, the secret beaches, the nooks and coves of my trade.

The height made me dizzy at first. Now thirst's taken over. At night, neither matter. Night's when the world goes black as the ocean depths, when the wind keens and the rust squeals and the dead whistle. I can't see you from up here, but I can smell the brine you bring with you. I can taste mouthfuls of wet sand. When it rains, the deluge feels like drowning. I cover my face, but the water finds a way in, every time.

My Mother's Ghosts

Priya Sharma

The dark and stormy night is welcome after the long, hot summer that's scorched the grass and put me in a stupor. I'm in a perpetual sweat. I lie awake through airless nights in my bedroom.

The violence of the storm breaks the tension and brings a kind of peace.

I am my mother's ghost and she is mine.

She follows me around the house. Right now, she's outside the toilet. I know this because her sigh penetrates everything, even my sleep. It verbalises her emotional exhaustion. She doesn't need words now that she has her powerful sigh. It creates a vacuum that sucks out all my feelings.

"Are you okay in there?" Her voice is low and slow. I pretend not to hear her.

"Charlotte?" There's a tentative knock.

"Go away."

"Charlotte, are they talking about us?"

She means in the village. I went out today for supplies, carting them back in my rucksack. Mum imagines the village as it was years ago, when her and

Dad bought this house. There was a butcher's, greengrocer's, post office and tearooms. A crucible for gossip.

I've tried to explain to Mum that I cut through the trees to the main road and walk the half mile to the supermarket. It's a great barn of a building in which to be anonymous.

Mum can't take it in. She's stuck in the past. I'm stuck in *her* past.

"Nobody's talking about us."

I wash my hands. When I open the door she's right outside, as if her nose was pressed against the wooden panelling.

People used to tell me that I'm a younger version of Mum. I wouldn't know. I've no idea what either of us look like.

Wash day is a chore. Mum has the demeanour of a beaten dog.

"I don't want to."

Her hair is lank and greasy, clumping in patches to reveal the thick flakes on her scalp. She used to spend hours in front of the mirror, doing her hair and makeup. We live in the country but Mum dressed like something from a film.

I bully Mum into the bath, pouring water over her head with a plastic measuring jug before she tries to climb out.

"The water's cold."

"It's the hottest I can get it." I push her back down.

Her crying makes me scrub harder. I stop when I realise that I'm raising red welts on her back.

"What will become of us? Who'll look after us?"

As if I've not been here my whole life doing exactly that. I must be strong so that she can be weak.

"Where's Jack?"

Now I want to scrub until I draw blood. To hold her head under the water, like she did to Arthur. He must have been terrified. At least Jack survived.

I sluice Mum down and wrap her in a towel instead. Action brings memory. I'm on this very spot, but time recedes to when the tiles were clean and whole, not cracked and mouldy. I'd wrap Arthur in a fluffy towel, warmed on the radiator. The one in my hands now is stiff and scratchy. I hope it takes her skin off.

Wherever Jack is now, at least he's out of it all.

"Come on, old man. It's your turn."

I unbutton his shirt and unzip his trousers.

"Get off me. You're young enough to be my daughter."

"Dad, please."

"Help! Get off me!"

I unbuckle the belts strapping him into his wheelchair so that I can undress him.

"Somebody help me!"

An unmistakeable smell rises from him. His pants are stained. He used to be able to tell me when he needed to go. I get him to stand but he grapples with me before I can get his Y-fronts down. There's still so much strength in those bony hands.

"Mum, calm him down, will you?"

She hovers, getting in the way without offering help. The heat's made her even more sluggish than normal. She moves so slowly that I want to shake her.

"Charlie." She takes his hand.

"Eva." The use of his last mistress' name used to make me furious.

The intricacies of the brain are alarming in their dysfunctions. Dad can see faces, his brain can process the image, but he can't remember whose face it is. I can see faces but can't process the image. The outcome's the same. Neither of us know who we're looking at.

Dad grasps Mum's forearms to steady himself. At least she calms him, if only for a little while. He puts his head close to hers.

"Penelope." He's correct this time. He kisses her cheek.

I gag as I wipe his smeared buttocks. You'd think I'd be used to it by now.

I sit in the armchair I've put beside the landing window, overlooking the drive. It's a nice spot. I get the last of the light. There's a stained-glass panel down the centre of the window, put in by a previous lord of the manor. It's of Demeter, arms laden with corn sheaves. I like the patches of colour it sheds on the floor and walls.

Bats flit through the warm twilight, feeding on the fly. Birds serenade the arrival of the night. I should feel settled, but something gnaws. I want to shrug myself off and become someone else.

I freeze. A flashlight's moving through the trees, a swinging line that lands on the defunct fountain in front of the house. Cars used to circle it, stopping to drop off party goers. The drive itself is wrecked, pot-holed and cracked by vicious winters, allowing new growth through it. The only access is from the main road and the gates have rusted shut.

The beam of light climbs up the front of the house. I duck out of sight. I wish I had a gun. I peep from behind the curtain, watching his progress. Everything about the figure marks it as male. It's confirmed when he stumbles and swears. A burglar would be stealthier.

Then he does the unthinkable. He comes up to the front door. The knocker lands on the wood with a series of heavy thuds.

A light goes on below. It must be Mum. I thought she was in bed. Running hurts my bare feet. They slap clumsily on the floor. Too late. She draws back the bolts as I reach the bottom step.

"Jack?" Mum says, then she collapses.

The man's as tall as me but broader. He drops the torch and sweeps Mum up. He manages her easily.

"Where shall I take her?"

"Up there."

He carries her up the stairs.

"That door." Mum's bedroom.

He's used the moment to take charge, kicking the door open with his foot and laying her on the bed. He smells of cigarette smoke. Wonderful in this house of decaying flesh.

Mum tips her head from side to side, her eyelids fluttering. "Jack?" She puts out a hand.

"It's okay, Mum." He hesitates over the final word. "You need to get some sleep."

"Will you be here when I wake up?"

"I promise."

She smiles, or something that passes for a smile.

I can see expressions and distinctive features but it's the face itself that's elusive. When I was younger and went out more, I used haircuts or clothes to recognise a person. Uniforms made negotiating school a nightmare, making me wary and shy. People thought I was stupid as I stared at them, trying to work out who they were.

Jack was young when he was taken into care. Too young to have a stance, a walk, or a gesture that would help me now. There was nothing on his face to mark him out. There are no vestiges of the boy I knew.

What I see now are sturdy legs, and sleeves rolled up to reveal knotted arms. Hair brushing his collar.

I close the door behind me so that Mum can't hear.

"Who are you?"

"It's me, Charlotte. Don't you recognise me? I'm Jack. I've come home."

The past is a hungry animal. It devours me, piecemeal.

Dad's a poor sleeper. Maybe it's because of his illness, or his guilty conscience. He's started wandering the corridors, which is punishing. I fret he'll fall and break something. When I'm too tired to supervise him, I tie him down and plug my ears against the shouts.

Tonight I let him roam. He shuffles along, stopping to pick at the wallpaper. I don't want to fall asleep with a stranger in the house. The man went straight up to Jack's room witho ut prompting. I should've made him leave right then.

"Penelope, what have you done with the children?"

"They're in bed." There's no point trying to correct him. "You shouldn't have left us like that, Dad."

Talking about it all now he's lost his mind isn't fair, but it makes me feel better to tell him what I couldn't when I was younger. I was scared of Dad. He was a stranger in our midst, who could destroy us all with a few words.

Now he stops and turns around. The way he looks at me makes my stomach lurch, but his clarity is short-lived.

"Where's Eva?"

"You phoned from the airport." Dad knew Mum never answered the phone. It brought on a panic attack. "You told me to tell Mum you were leaving with Eva. You said, 'Promise you'll look after them, Charlotte. They'll never cope without you. They need you.'"

"Jack, Jack, Jack" raps on the wall as he walks along.

"Before you hung up you said, 'You can love someone too much.' What did you mean?"

Love hurts. That's what he meant. I resolved not to love anymore as I put the receiver back in its cradle.

Dad gets away from me. He raps at the first door he comes to. It opens and our uninvited guest is in the doorway, rubbing his face.

"Jack, Jack, Jack," Dad says.

My favourite time of day is before anyone else is awake. The house is pleasant this way. The quarry tiles in the kitchen are cool underfoot. Everything is quiet.

I make a pot of tea and take a cup to Mum. Her legs stick out from under the sheet, skin flaking all over the bed and carpet. I arrange the pillows behind her as she sits up. As I lean over her, I smell something sour in her morning-breath.

Drawing the curtains shows the room up. One wall is lined with framed images from her photoshoots. Her dressing table is thick with dust. The perfumes are stale. The potions separating in their glass jars. The prongs of her hairbrush are clogged with dirty hair

"Mum, is it really Jack?"

She looks past me. I hate that. It's like she's seen someone behind. I seize her chin and turn her head in my direction. There's a delay before her gaze follows.

"Yes."

"How can you be sure?"

"I'm sure."

She's suddenly forbidding and formidable. Then, after she's stared me down, come great gusts of self-indulgent sobs. A confusing contrast.

Yes, there she is. The mother I grew up with.

There's nothing for it. I slip a kitchen knife into my pocket and go up to where would-be-Jack is sleeping.

I used to clean Jack's room when I had time. He was

fascinated by animal bones. Birds. Small mammals. Each specimen was labelled in his childish hand with its Latin name, where and when he found it.

Mum wrinkled up her nose at his collection. *You little psychopath.* It was one of the few things she found funny.

Except it wasn't so funny when Jack punched Arthur until he sobbed. Mum put Jack out in the rain as punishment. He stood, face against the window, watching Mum pretending to read by the fire. Neither of them would give in. Dad broke the deadlock when he came home.

For God's sake, Penelope, do you want him to get pneumonia?

Dad picked him up and carried him in, Jack's smile triumphant over Dad's shoulder.

Is this Jack?

I stand in the door. The sheet's pushed down to the man's waist. Light brown hair covers his upper chest. Everything about him is lean and long. He's an undernourished wolf.

"Get up."

I open the curtains and sun floods the bed.

"How did you get that?"

There's a long scar along his left collarbone. He touches it, as if he's forgotten it, then laughs.

"You'd be shocked by my life, sis."

There's a hardness to him that makes me think, *Yes, you might be Jack after all.*

I reach out and run my forefinger along the irregular, thick line. His lips part, just a fraction.

"You could be as beautiful as Mum was, if you took care of yourself."

Mum was a model. People joked that Dad, who inherited a fortune from a German uncle, chose her from a magazine.

The man flings back the sheet and I look away.

Life's suddenly uncertain. The only thing I can rely on is routine. So-called-Jack offers to help. I let him.

He shaves Dad and then feeds him breakfast, coaxing him with spoon after spoon, long after I've lost patience. He wipes the porridge from Dad's chin with a gentleness that I can't second-guess. Would real-Jack be so kind?

Mum sits in the chair opposite and stares. She eats like the food's choking her.

"What next?" Jack asks.

"Wheel him out onto the patio for a dose of morning sun while I pick some food."

If this weather doesn't break soon everything I've planted will die. I take a colander out to the rose bed, now filled with peas. They're starting to wither, the leaves yellowing, like the grass. The sun is bleaching the colour from the world. I peel a pod at intervals to taste the tender greenness nestling within.

When I look up, Jack's knelt beside Dad's chair. He talks to Dad, but he's watching me. Then he comes over.

"You've done a good job here." He helps me pick.

"It's not picturesque, but I like it."

"I'm not talking about the garden."

I know what he meant but he can go to hell if he thinks his opinion matters. He responds to my silence with, "This used to be full of flowers."

"Yes, Mum and Dad were all about the spectacle."

Before Dad's dalliances and Mum went off her rocker there were guests that stayed for weekends. Staff were brought in for parties that went on all night. Where are those free-loading champagne-guzzlers now?

The girls at school used to call me *New Money* and snigger. They mocked my parents for buying the old hall and playing at being the landed gentry. Their mothers looked away, embarrassed, when they saw me pushing Arthur in his pram. They'd mutter to each other or give me a patronising smile. *They're so happy, Down's children, aren't they?*

No, they're just children, like yours. They cry. They laugh.

I wanted to tear their faces off.

The memories still smart. I want Jack, if he is Jack, to leave it all alone, but he doesn't. I'm not sure what bothers me more - the subject or that it's proof that he *is* Jack. And that maybe that I don't want him to be.

"Dad called us a bunch of headcases."

"Well, he's one too now, isn't he?"

"When did he come home?"

"A few years after Mum was released. Eva didn't want a man with dementia."

Sad, really. I think Dad really loved her. Or at least more than he loved us.

"So the old goat dragged his carcass back here."

"Mum was glad to see him." I was too.

The colander's full now. I have to ask him.

"What do you remember about that day?"

If this is Jack, he'll know exactly what I'm talking about.

"You and Mum were fighting. I'd never seen you so angry. Mum started with her normal stuff."

You're not safe out there. All you have is us. No-one will love you like we do. People will laugh at you. They'll hurt you.

"But you wouldn't have it, Charlotte. You wanted to go out. Mum was crying, saying you were going to leave us because of Arthur, just like Dad did. Where were you going that was so important?"

"I went for a walk. I just wanted to be alone for a while." My mouth contorts. I should be crying now. My heart should be in tatters but there's a place beyond tears, pleasure or love. It's the sanctuary of the ultimate safety and despair. "Dad didn't leave because of Arthur. He left for Eva."

We tell ourselves the most outrageous lies.

"Arthur was screaming. He wouldn't stop. You were the only person who could comfort him, but you didn't because you were furious at Mum."

There's no reproach in his voice. There should be. I could've picked Arthur up. Soothed him. I went for a walk instead and Mum drowned him in the bath.

Well, I did ask. It serves me right.

Mum's come outside. She stands, clutching one handle of Dad's wheelchair. Her gaze is unfocused. She sways. She'd stand there forever if I let her. Dad's chatting to himself and plucking at the fabric of his trousers.

We go in for lunch. Jack pushes Dad, flanked by Mum, her step hesitant and faltering. I bring up the rear. Here we are, me and my fucked-up family.

❖

"Help me bring the chickens in."

It's dusk. Jack and I head out to the part of the garden overlooked by the drawing room. The chickens scratch around out here by day, coming and going through the long doors. They've decimated the lawn.

Jack throws his head back, bellowing with laughter.

"Bloody hell. *We* weren't allowed in there."

We herd the chickens in. The green room used to be a calm space. The green silk moire wallpaper shimmered in the sun, making the room a lagoon. Mum loved it. Maybe that's why I let the chickens defile it. One wall was soaked after a pipe broke and now verdant mould blooms on the peeling paper. All I care about are fresh eggs.

I like the chickens too. They recognise me. I like the warmth of their breasts through their feathers and their throaty clucks as I stroke them. My affections are pragmatic. I'm not above killing and skinning one.

Jack can't stop laughing as they roost on bookshelves and in open drawers.

"Just wait until you have to shovel out the shit and feathers."

We're both laughing now, fit to bring tears to my eyes. I can't remember when I last laughed with someone. I'm overcome with the urge to reach out and embrace him.

Jack reaches below a chicken and pulls out an egg.

"This is cause for a celebration. Do you have any whisky, sis?"

❖

The library was Dad's favourite room, just as the green drawing room was Mum's. I associate it with the smell of cigars and men's laughter from those weekend-long parties.

The books in here were bought with the house. Rows of encyclopaedias, reference manuals, the classics in leather binding, art books and atlases. I daren't remove the ones on the far bookshelves in case they're holding the wall up.

Jack sloshes whisky into heavy crystal tumblers after rinsing them out. It's never occurred to me to try some. It was Dad's drink. I take a sniff, then a slug. It's antiseptic and scalding. Jack sits back, cradling the glass in his hands. It's gone unsaid that I've accepted he's Jack.

"I wanted to stay here with you when they arrested Mum."

"That's funny. You never seemed to need me when you were little."

He never seemed to need anyone. Our mother doesn't feature in this parenting equation.

"Not true. I always wanted you but you were too busy with Arthur when he came along."

"Arthur needed me more. And I was never going to get custody of you. I was only eighteen, and with my condition..." I sound like I'm justifying myself. "The only reason I was allowed to stay here myself was Mr Baines."

Mr Baines, Dad's solicitor. A dull, solid man who helped me with bills and tradesmen.

"Your condition." Jack waggles his forefinger at his own face. "You seem to manage okay now."

"Barely."

I've been called maladjusted, misfit, personality disordered, and fucking weirdo. I think Dad was the most relieved when a private neuropsychiatrist diagnosed a form of propognosia. Face blindness.

At least she's not retarded.

On the contrary, your daughter's exceptionally bright.

"Why didn't Dad come home? I kept asking for him."

"He was in India with Eva, searching for enlightenment in an ashram in the middle of nowhere. Nobody could find him."

We fall silent. A fly skitters along the wall, high up, out of swatting range. My emotions are up there too, buzzing.

"This is expensive stuff. It's from Japan." Jack picks up the bottle of whisky and examines the label. "They had the best of everything, didn't they?"

"So?" I don't know why I'm so defensive.

"I didn't understand that we were loaded when I was a kid."

"What's your point?"

"I've seen a very different side of life to you." He strokes the scar on his collarbone.

"Yes, because my life's *so* easy." I spit the words at him.

"It's all relative."

"Where exactly have you been all this time, Jack? I wrote to you. Every week. You never wrote back. You refused to see me. Then you disappeared."

"I was angry."

"That's it? You were angry?"

"Yes. Angry at all of you. None of you wanted me."

You can't negotiate with pain, so I don't even try.

"So what's changed?"

"There's stuff I've done, bad things, to survive. I'm in trouble. I need to lie low."

"For God's sake..."

"It's okay. They won't look for me here."

The buzzing fly's incessant in its futile rage. There's a band of grey clouds in the distance, sucking the light out of the sky. They bleed dark lines into the trees below.

"Tomorrow. You go tomorrow."

He sighs, as if he expected this reaction.

"Do you remember the flour bin?"

The change of subject throws me.

"Yes."

We'd gone into the pantry to steal biscuits. The narrow space was cold and dark, lit by a single bare bulb. It was lined by shelves, stacked with boxes and cans. The flour bin was large, with a loose lid. It sat on the floor beside a drum of cooking oil.

There was a rapid thudding inside the bin, followed by silence. Then the thudding started again, followed by a high-pitched squeal. Jack and I looked at one another.

"We pulled back the lid." Jack drained his glass. "There were three rats inside."

"One was a gnawed carcass." I continue the story for him. "One was thrashing around, blood on his neck."

"And the third one was sleek and healthy," he finished pointedly.

I wonder what Jack means by reminding me of this salutary lesson in survival.

❖

I'm the last to have a bath. I step out, dripping and shivering. The house is cooling rapidly as the storm approaches.

"Damn!"

The floor's still wet from the struggle with Dad. I slip, calling out as I go down. I try and breathe through the shock, taking an inventory of what hurts.

"Are you okay?"

Jack's right outside the door. The flimsy bolt pops off. I snatch at my towel, trying to cover myself.

"Get out."

"Sorry. I thought you were hurt."

"I'm fine. Just winded." I wince as I move. "Pass me my bathrobe."

He hands it to me, bunched up in his fist, then turns around very slowly. I tie the robe's belt, aware of my body – my unloved, untouched body – beneath the thin cotton.

"Let's get you up."

He slips his arm under mine. There's a distant rumbling.

"One, two, three."

His heat seeps into me. He takes my weight easily. His t-shirt is cut away at the neck. Of all life's mysteries, sex is the one that we can experience every day if we choose. Except for me. The only mystery I'm acquainted with is death.

"I can manage."

I draw away when we reach my bedroom door. My thigh's throbbing. I landed heavily. Jack follows me in, shutting the door behind him. When I sit down on the bed, he kneels beside me and takes my leg in his hands, pushing at the bone from calf to thigh. His fingers are on my inner thigh, close to my most private place.

"Nothing's broken but you'll have an almighty bruise tomorrow."

He sits beside me on the bed. His pregnant pause is leading up to something.

"I'm worried about you, Charlotte. You can't carry on looking after Mum and Dad on your own. You're run ragged."

"You won't talk me into letting you stay."

"Just hear me out. They need proper care. A nursing home and specialists. When was the last time Mum saw a psychiatrist? And the house, the whole thing needs rewiring and replumbing."

"We've only got enough to see us from month to month."

"Where did all the money go?"

"We've been living on it."

"Even in this state, the house is still worth something. And the land. You could sell it."

"I don't know. Mum and Dad wouldn't want that."

"Do you think they'd want you living like *this?* What do *you* want, Charlotte?"

I've never been asked that before. "I don't know."

"Fuck." He shakes his head, like something's tearing loose in him. "I can't do this anymore. I'm not your brother. Sorry."

"I don't understand."

"We shared a squat. Jack knew this guy, said he'd give us both work. Stuff you don't want to know about. Jack used to talk about you. About what happened."

"I don't believe you."

The thunder's getting closer. I'm shaken to my foundations.

"It's the truth."

"Then where's Jack?"

"We both got greedy. Our boss caught up with Jack. I only came here because I had nowhere else to go. I was only going to stay for a few days." He reaches out for my hand. I pull away. "We could go somewhere. Just the two of us."

There's a flash of light.

"Don't tell me, you were looking for somewhere to hide but now you've fallen in love with me."

"We both need a new start. We need each other."

This pulls me up short because it's the truth, whoever he is.

"How can I trust you?"

The air crackles. The distance between us is charged. "Would I do *this* if I were Jack?"

He reaches out and cradles my face in his hands. His thumb strokes the skin beneath my ears. It's not the touch of a brother for his sister. He leans in. The involuntary sound of yearning escapes my lips.

What surprises me most is the tenderness. No, this can't be Jack.

I need to check on Dad. I put him to bed before I had my bath, buckling him to the wrought iron bedframe for safety.

Mum's hovering outside the door. Always hovering.

"You're dad's crying. He's scared of the storm."

Not *Charles*. Not *my husband*. He's my responsibility. She abdicated long ago.

Mum peers into the darkness behind me. At the bare leg tangled in the blanket. Then her head swivels, taking in my nakedness beneath the robe. Her movements are slow and her eyes look blank, but she's assembling these pieces. I close the bedroom door.

Her mouth's downturned. The rain's hammering on the roof, pouring from the broken gutter onto the front of the house. It feels like it'll never stop.

"He's not Jack," I whisper. "He's—"

I don't know his name.

The door behind me opens with a click. He's there, bare-chested, doing up the buttons of his jeans' fly. A visceral thrill shoots through me. My face burns.

"Tell her," Mum says. There's a thunderclap.

"Tell her what?"

The lightning flash illuminates the hall's stained-glass panel. We're directly below the tempest. It's a timeless drama played out on a greater scale than ours.

"You're Jack. Tell her."

"You're crazy." He sounds uncertain.

"I know you, you little psychopath."

"No."

"I lied for you. I should've told them."

"About what?" I ask, even though I'm scared of the answer.

"You're a confused old woman."

"Tell her about Arthur."

I look from one of them to the other.

"Tell Charlotte," Mum musters all the venom she can, "or I will."

Her anger still has power. He throws up his hands. "I told you before. Arthur wouldn't stop crying. You left me and he wouldn't shut up."

"What did you do?" I sound as slow as Mum.

"He liked having a bath. I was trying to calm him down. It was an accident."

It's like he's explaining how he broke a toy. Arthur was fully dressed when I pulled him out of the water, his sodden clothes flooded my lap. Jack wasn't giving him a bath.

"You knew exactly what you were doing."

"I thought you'd walked out on us, just like Dad. I thought you weren't coming back."

I cover my mouth with my hands. The lightning feels biblical. It's true. It's all true and the whole world has changed. Jack killed Arthur. I slept with Jack. No amount of rain will wash this away.

Jack reads me like a book.

"The rules don't apply to you and me. This doesn't have to change anything." He reaches out for me. "We can start again. Be anybody we want."

I shove him away. We're both disgusting.

"I know you. I saw your face when you found Arthur. You were relieved."

Promise you'll look after them, Charlotte. They'll never cope without you. They need you.

All I wanted to do was walk in the woods for a few hours. Mum, Jack and Arthur were so heavy. Mum's tears filled up my lungs. I couldn't breathe.

"Don't pretend, Charlotte. You're as guilty—"

I want to shut Jack up. I slam his head against the wall as hard as I can.

"Mum, will you stay with Jack while I see to Dad?"

"Yes."

Mum and I hold vigil by Jack's bed. I've cleaned the boggy swelling on the side of his skull as best as I can. We listen to his ragged breath. His lips are dry and cracked.

"Why didn't you tell me, Mum?"

"I didn't want to ruin the rest of Jack's life. It was my fault."

"We're all to blame."

I don't feel angry at her for weeping. Not this time. "If anyone comes, Charlotte, I'll tell them this was me."

She means what happened to Jack. Her hand hovers over my arm but she can't bring herself to touch me. It's okay. It's enough. I start to cry. Is your mother meant to be the person who breaks your heart? She looks so small and vulnerable.

If she's my mother, then I'm hers too.

Jack wakes up on the third day. His eyelids flutter, then open. The moan coming from his mouth doesn't sound human. One of his eyes is pulled up in a different direction to the other, marking his intracranial derangement.

Yes, we're a bunch of headcases.

The air in the room is cool and bright. The days have felt calm after the storm.

Jack's hand shakes as he lifts it to my cheek. His single word is mauled and elongated, but I understand it: "Mum."

Old Women and Knives

Phil Sloman

It was a dark and stormy night. Wind-whipped rains savaged the stone of the cottage, threatening to find a way inside. *It's raining old women and knives, boy, that's* what Bryn's father would have said, God rest his soul. The years were long gone since anyone had called Bryn 'boy', and those who had were cold and rotting in the grave.

Bryn threw another log on the fire.

The cottage was its own grave of sorts. Isolated and abandoned, with visitors few and far between. What visitors he did have dwindled in the months after Annie's passing. Most came in the first few weeks with well-meaning handshakes alongside words of condolence. Idle empty phrases meant more to fill the silence than anything else. In the end they had all drifted away, and now it was the silence which spoke to Bryn most. The silence and her.

Bryn settled back into his chair with one eye to the shadows.

"Leave me alone now, you hear!"

Bryn's words echoed back at him from the darkness. He shivered, putting one hand to the tired skin of his throat. The coals were dying in the hearth. How long had it been this time? An hour? Two? More? Outside the winds continued to howl their pain. *Old women and knives* he thought to himself and shivered again.

The dream was always the same.

Black dots wheeled back and forth on the breeze across a cloudless sky, ravens in search of easy pickings. He stood alone in the field, his cap held in both hands, twisting it back and forth as if wringing out a dishcloth.

"I'm sorry, my love."

Except there was no one living to hear those words. Only the black rectangle of nothing dug into the ground, six feet deep and half as narrow.

"Why?" The word whispered on the breeze, almost lost among the ripple of the grasses.

"It was for the best."

"For who?"

And he didn't answer. He didn't know how.

"For who?" Except this time there was a force to the words, an anger whipping up the winds. Overhead the sky was darkening, black cloud blossoming across the ether, blotting out the sun. And the winds grew, stronger and stronger. Enough to unsteady him, to force him to take a step forward, and another.

"No, Annie. No. Please." He struggled to make his words heard above the storm, the wind a pressing wall behind him as he fought to back away from the grave. Black darts struck from above, feathered terrors clawing and gouging, disorientating him.

"Leave me alone now, you hear!" Always those words.

Then he was falling forward, into the hole, falling deeper and deeper and deeper, falling into her arms.

In the cottage, Bryn stared into the darkness and thought about putting another log on the fire.

Bryn pulled the blanket tighter around him. If he ignored it, it might go away.

There had been no dreams this time, simply a welcome void of emptiness. Almost calming. He'd awoken into darkness with the fire long dead, the cottage in silence. Except it wasn't. There was a sound coming from the kitchen, faint and almost unnoticed. Metronomic. And that was what made him pull the blanket closer.

Thud, thud, thud.

Bryn grimaced. The springs and fabric of the chair adjusting as he shifted his weight, the leather creaking in the stillness of the room. There was a table beside him, and on the table was a lamp. He reached out in the darkness with uncertain hands, afraid of what he might touch. Or what might touch him.

She'd grabbed him once. Or so he had thought. In the dark. He'd screamed, long and loud, except no one came running. There wasn't anyone to hear. Bryn had sat in the dark, rocking back and forth until the sun came up. But he knew she would come back. She always did.

His hand touched metal and a scattering of matches. The shadows retreated as a matchhead flared, the flame holding steady for the lamp, biting at the wick. Perhaps that would be the end of it.

Thud, thud, thud.

Bryn recoiled. The banging was louder this time.

Insistent. The lamp wobbled on the table, threatening to fall to the hard wooden floor underneath, then steadied. Bryn breathed deeply, his fingers gripping the arms of the chair. His eyes scanned left to right, looking for anything in the shadows that shouldn't be there. Anything unnatural.

Thud, thud, thud.

"Christ, please," he croaked, knowing his prayers would not be heard this time. Religion had been instilled in him when he was a boy by his Da. Sunday's always for the Lord, with prayers to be said before food and bedtime every day. The Lord forgives sinners, he'd been taught, except sometimes the sin was too great.

He was also taught that cowards would burn in hell.

Bryn pushed back against the chair, rising, then falling as his body betrayed him, before rising again on unsteady legs, using the table for support. Arthritis screamed in his joints and he had to stop, counting the seconds until it subsided. It was a moment more before he could pick up the lamp.

Around the room the shadows moved, retreating and advancing as the lamp swung in his grip. Bryn crossed himself, trying to remember the last time he had made it to church. He had visited once since the funeral, but he'd promised not to go again. There had been eyes on him all the time he was there. Members of the congregation judging him, at least in his mind, whispering behind their hymn books even though they couldn't know what he had done. Now he wished he hadn't been so foolish.

Thud, thud, thud.

Bryn grimaced and looked to the kitchen. His cane

was by the chair, and he picked it up as much for reassurance as to aid his steps. The head was rounded and polished from too many years of use, the tip capped with metal. It had been his Da's, and it had tasted Bryn's rump more than it had been used for support. He was more grateful for its presence now than he ever had been back when his Da was alive.

Cold air and fine spray hit him as he opened the kitchen door. Bryn raised the lamp high, letting the light bleed into the dark recesses. The room was compact, built purely for function – narrow cupboards set at head height; a small table and chairs hard up against the far wall; a large stove on the other, black and coated with grease. Directly in front of him was the sink, the ceramic cracked, dirty dishes piled high on the draining board where he had left them unwashed. To the left of the sink was the door, and beyond the door was the storm and miles of empty fields. The kitchen window was set above the sink, large and imposing; it usually provided views of the distant hills beyond, but tonight they were lost in darkness. The window was swinging freely, the latch hanging limply as the elements played with the window, banging it repeatedly into the rotting wooden frame.

He had shut the window in the daytime. He was sure of it. But now... Bryn set the lamp down on the table along with his cane. The chair scraped across the floorboards as he dragged it from table to sink. Cold spray peppered his face as he clambered on to the seat, one cautious foot after the other, a hand to the sink for balance. Leaning forward, Bryn grabbed at the rain-slick latch, pulling the window to. Up close he could see the glass had fractured, ill-conceived spider webs devoid of beauty or function spreading across the pane. His own reflection stared back, mirrored in the blackness of the outside world, tired and broken. The fields beyond were lost to him in the dark, no doubt flooded or close to it. He wondered how much rain they had soaked up and how much more they could take. Annie had been alive the last time the fields were drowned. She'd worked with Bryn to clean the cottage after the storm, removing layers of filth from where the waters had reached their highpoint. He looked to the kitchen wall, to a faded line which was somewhere around his waistline.

"Better get the towels," he sighed to himself, taking one last look out the window. Annie stared back at him, opening her mouth far wider than God had intended. Screeching, birthing an eruption of sound, forcing the glass to shatter inwards.

Bryn pushed back from the worktop, the chair tottering beneath him. It balanced improbably on two legs for a second, then one, twisting like a marionette before giving way. He heard the crack first, a gunshot of a sound, sharp and loud, then the pain consumed him. A thousand needles jabbing at his hip with savage intensity, his bones grinding together at unintended angles, shards of glass piercing his flesh. Bryn's face paled, becoming yellowed and ashen.

Between the flashes of pain, he pictured Annie's fractured face staring from the darkness before everything shattered. She was gaunt, far thinner than when she was alive, her cheekbones picked out in detail beneath paper-thin skin. Wispy grey strands of hair plastered her scalp, while her mouth hung open in accusation. Her teeth were rotten, a mixture of yellows and black, unmarked tombstones half-concealing a throat filled with dirt and worms.

"Annie," he whimpered, hot tears streaking his cheeks. "Annie, I'm sorry."

The darkness swallowed him.

The ravens circled overhead, chasing across the clear blue skies. Bryn picked at the fabric of his cap, plucking with his fingers at the fibres as he twisted it in his hands. The view was different this time. Seen from underneath. Distorted. A rectangle of blue above him with no panorama, nor fields, nor grave.

Specks of rain came unannounced, finding their way to his cheeks in the depths of the hole, the sky bruising above him, turning from blue to grey to black. At first there was one spot of rain then another; slow, inconsistent. Then a deluge. Fat drops of water cascading from above, feeding the ground until it was engorged, and dirty earth-tainted water dripped from the sides of the grave to pool around his broken form.

Clods of earth collapsed on top of him as the grave crumbled. Bryn clawed at the sides, trying to get to standing, screaming in hope and desperation. His chest tightened as the waters rose and the earth fell, his ribs constricting, forcing the air from his lungs. Whispered words found their way to his ears; all unintelligible. He lifted his head, straining to see down the length of his body in the growing dark. What looked like thin roots ensnared him, brittle wood creeping over the width of his chest, moving, adjusting their grip, dragging him down into the soft earth. Roots with fingertips and nails and a wedding ring he'd once proposed with, when his knees would bend, and his heart was lighter.

Words whispered in his ear once more and this time he heard them more clearly than anything in his life.

"Together. Forever."

The lamplight had died down, little more than the glow of a will-o'-the-wisp lost in the dark and the rain. The rains had continued while Bryn remained corpse-like, new-born streams running down the hills and drowning the fields, with only one place to collect; all around Bryn was water and distorted shadows rippling in the dying lamplight.

Bitter water flooded into his open mouth bringing with it hair and grit and slivers of glass. Bryn coughed violently, lost between reality and his dreams, fighting to breathe, brown liquid spilling over his lips and into his nicotine-yellowed stubble. The rest he swallowed, an uncomfortable cocktail of filth and disease sucked down deep inside his body. More water fought to enter his mouth, eager to fill the space around his tongue and teeth. He gagged, spewing out more muck, pushing to prop himself up on his elbows with his head above water. He screamed as his body rebelled, pain tearing through his broken hip. His arms gave way and he collapsed backwards, his head thumping into the floor through the water. Something slithered around him unseen.

Once more, water flooded his mouth, tasting of despair. Bryn wanted to swallow and be done with it, to choke down the ice-cold liquid until his lungs burnt and his world ended. To be free. Of her. Of the guilt.

"Not yet."

The roots of his hair erupted in pain across the numbed surface of his scalp, clawed fingers grabbing handfuls of wiry grey strands, dragging his head above the water. He vomited rancid liquid from his mouth, from his nostrils. Snot and water and blood dirtying his stubble, his breathing ragged, his heart racing.

The plop of earth falling into water sounded behind him, coupled with a retching noise; the same sound Annie had made the night she had died, the contents of her stomach spilling into the bucket he held to her mouth as he breathed in the stench of her death. Each splash here and now made him want to look backwards, to see her once more, and with each splash he begged for his heart to give out.

"Annie," he burbled through a mouth filled with snot and tears, though he didn't know if the tears were for her or for himself. Great clumps of hair dragged free of his scalp, exposing open sores left to bleed into the darkness with no one to see. No one to help.

"Not yet."

His hair slackened as she released him, letting his head slump backwards into a soft mound of cold wet earth. Worms writhed within the mound, cavorting with beetles and millipedes and the other carrion-devourers beneath the ground. Bryn felt their twitching movement under the weave of his hair, the scurrying feet of insects running unseen all over him. He imagined mandibles finding the fresh soft flesh of his scalp where the wounds were ripe, biting eagerly and deep. Would he feel it? Or would they start to burrow further inside him, biting and digging until they had wormed their way down to the bone?

Water rippled to his left.

Her nightgown dragged in the muck, trailing in her wake as she glided across the floor. Bryn hadn't seen her move like that in years: tall, upright, with purpose. Unrecognisable from the woman who died in his bed. Shrivelled had been the word the undertaker had used. Bryn hadn't been meant to hear them say that, muttered over a smouldering cigarette outside the window, colleague to colleague. But he had, and he hadn't disagreed. In his heart he knew he'd thought worse. A broken husk. Better off dead. It was for the best.

"For who?"

"You're not real. You're just in my head." The words trembled from his throat, weak and unconvincing in the half-light. The rains continued to fall outside. "You're not real!"

Annie turned on him, contorting her body, her head facing him before her torso followed, her legs still twisted toward the wall. The force of her was on top of him before he realised, the stench of the grave filling his nostrils, peaty and rich and decaying. Her mouth enveloped his, kissing him like when they were teenagers but without the passion, her tongue probing, violent. But not her tongue. Something else from deep inside her. A deformation of worms, plump and conjoined, twisted around one another to form a pulsing muscle in his mouth, suffocating him.

"*I. Am. Real!*" Even now, with her mouth clamped to his, he could hear her clearly. "*Swallow.*"

"Swallow." That is what he had said to her that night. "Swallow. Every last drop. The doctor said it would make you feel better." And she had. Every last drop. It was meant to be quick and painless. It was what he gave to the diseased livestock all those years ago before the markets collapsed. "Cheaper than a bolt to the head, boy," his Da used to say.

"*Swallow,*" she hissed. And he did, letting the worms slide down his throat, feeling them burst apart from each other inside him, churning in his stomach amongst the acid and bile. He vomited.

But they weren't done. The waters around him erupted in a seething mass of agitation, the worms multiplying, splitting and growing, birthing more creatures, blind and searching, eager to find the warmth of Bryn's insides again. Bryn screamed, pushing back with his arms, trying to keep his head above the water, shrieking as his hip sang out in agony, but he kept going, pushing beyond the pain, beyond the hysteria, desperate to escape the madness.

"*Stay!*"

Bryn's hand slipped on the scum-slickened floorboards hidden beneath the rainwater. For a second, he found purchase with his elbow then he collapsed, his head submerging once again. Bloodthirsty ribbons of flesh surged forwards, hunting for an opening, moving with the ferocity of piranhas, finding passage within his nostrils, his ears, his tear ducts. Bryn's head broke the surface, gasping for air. He could feel the creatures inside him, burrowing deeper, devouring the soft tissue of his insides, the sensation numb and distant. Even now, though, his instinct was to escape, to backpedal away from the waters and the nightmares.

He looked for Annie, needing to know where she was, what was planned for him next. To plead with her for forgiveness. Except she was gone. He looked behind him, needing to be certain, expecting to see her there ready with some new torture, but all he could see were shadows. She was surely hiding there somewhere... but around him the waters fumed with creatures, and he didn't care anymore. If she wanted him, she would take him. For now, he had to get out of the rising flood before he drowned, or worse.

Hand after hand, he dragged himself onwards across the floor, moving to the internal door where the floor was higher, grimacing with each jolt of movement. In the darkness it looked like the door was shut. Had he done that? It didn't matter. Either way it was a blessing, a barrier against the flooding and the creatures. A couple more feet and he would be there...

He sensed rather than saw the ripple of water at his feet, a different movement to the creatures. Something controlled. The touch was gentle at first, a loving caress. The tender stroke of flesh against flesh, like lovers exploring each other. Then the touch changed, became more forceful. Pain encircled his ankle as greedy fingers grasped him firmly, dragging him further away from his imagined safety. Bryn screeched and then his head slumped under the surface.

"Stay!"

The knife was in him before he could fight back, before he could sit up for air. The blade was long and sharp, aggressive, violating him, cutting through the muscle of his shoulder and out the other side. Annie pushed hard into the handle, her face up close to Bryn's as the tip bit deep into the floorboards.

"Stay."

Pain flared in his left shoulder as more steel was driven into the soft wood beneath him and the water filled his mouth and lungs.

"It's for the best."

For who? he thought. *For who?*

Outside, the rains continued to pour.

Errol

Paul M. Feeney

It *should* have been a dark and stormy night, but it wasn't.

Not even close.

Sure, it *was* night, the cloudless sky peppered with pinpricks of starlight and a slice of bright moon, but the air was still and quiet. Even the mid-winter chill that had bitten harshly over the last few days was absent, though it was still cold enough.

Not that Gordon Price could feel it.

Hurtling southbound on the A1 at just a shade over the limit in his top-of-the-range BMW, he had the environmental controls blasting out warmth *and* had the heat-seater on, making the leather upholstery nice and toasty. Just how he preferred it. It was as comfortable as one might wish, especially for someone who felt the cold a little too keenly, despite his extra padding.

Yet Gordon wasn't all that relaxed; not as much as he would like, anyway. He *should* have been in his sitting-room, a tumbler of whisky clutched in one hand, a cigar in the other. Instead, he was driving down one of Britain's shittiest roads in the dead hours of the night. Luckily, there didn't appear to be much in the way of other vehicles abroad; he hadn't even seen one of the usually ubiquitous lorries, either passing him on the northbound lane or holding him up on his side.

Outside, the landscape consisted solely of bare, skeletal trees and scraggly bushes. The bleak vista, rendered in shades of grey, was the only thing reflective of Gordon's dark mood. Trust the weather to be completely lacking in dramatic flair. Of course, he mused wryly, later he might very well have cause to be grateful for the relatively mild climate.

It was all Brenda's fault.

It usually was, as far as Gordon was concerned. Years of needling and nagging and constant whining had finally broken through his saintly patience (as he saw it) and he had snapped, allowing his pent-up rage (something he usually channelled down *other* avenues) to flow. The fight – admittedly one-sided, for Brenda had soon shut up in the face of his fury, and quite right too, the stupid cow – had escalated until...

But Gordon turned his thoughts away from the culmination of their conflict. He didn't want to spoil his new-found feelings of freedom, his tentative – and therefore, as yet, alien – sense of release. It was a strange situation he now found himself in, though one he knew he would come to appreciate. Relish, even. But first, he had to take care of one final piece of business, and it was this that was preventing him from fully relaxing.

A stretch of winding road caused Gordon to slow, but when it straightened out again, he didn't speed up. He was close to his destination. The turn-off he wanted was only a back road and might easily be missed. He hadn't been this way in years.

There.

Coming up, indicated by a signpost for places called 'Markham' and 'Hillington', was the junction. He swung the big motor into its dark mouth without slowing, the rear end sliding with momentum, before it righted when he stomped down on the accelerator.

Nearly there.

If his teenage memories weren't deceiving him, this road would eventually lead down near a smallish wood, a copse of trees that he and a group of friends had stumbled upon one drunken afternoon many years before, and where they had continued their revelry until darkness had begun to fall and the hush had crept upon their nerves. A gulf of decades separated that day from now, yet Gordon had never forgotten the isolation he'd felt, nor the sense of untouched wildness. Though the wood wasn't too far from this road, he had the impression that few – if any – people ever went there. Certainly neither he nor his friends had ever suggested going back.

Until now. That was where he intended to divest himself of the burden in his boot.

The big car rumbled along the road, passing numerous junctions leading off into the black. At one point he passed another sign for somewhere called 'Greenmarsh' and vaguely remembered there was a military base of some kind in the area.

When he felt he might be near his destination, Gordon slowed the vehicle to search for the turn-off he needed, and it was only this that prevented the car from veering off into one of the fields when something smashed into the back of it.

As it was, the BMW still spun out, Gordon fighting uselessly with the steering-wheel until it came to a stop facing back the way he'd come from.

He sat, shocked, fingers curled tight around the leather, making it creak, foot jammed hard against the brake.

What the fuck was that?

An animal of some kind; a cow or large deer at least, no doubt, to have caused such an impact.

Gordon slammed his fists down on the steering-wheel. "Blast and bugger! Fuck!"

He sat for a few moments more.

Then he sighed and, after yanking up the handbrake with that ratcheting noise he loved so much, cracked open the driver's door. He turned off the engine and removed the keys with the blind habit of an action taken thousands of times.

Immediately, cool air from outside stole in, feeling uncomfortably chilly in contrast to the warmth of the enclosed interior; a warmth that was now rapidly dissipating. Gordon heaved himself out, breathing hard for such a small effort, and slammed the door behind him.

Maybe it's time I started exercising more, change my diet.

He filed the thought away for later, then went to inspect the damage.

It was worse than he'd anticipated.

The entire panel on the back-passenger side was dented and scraped, and the back-bumper was hanging off at the corner. It also looked as though the rear wheel was slightly out of alignment, though Gordon couldn't be sure; the damage might just be making it seem that way.

Regardless, the more he looked at it, the angrier he got. What the *hell* could have done this? And just where the fuck was it?

Gordon looked around but couldn't see any obvious culprit. No body or injured beast (which he would have liked, as it would have given him something to take his ire out on). And no sign of damage to the bushes bordering road and fields. Though there were no streetlights, there was enough ambient illumination from the stars and strip of moon for his eyes to pick out grey detail close by. He doubted whatever had done this was hiding in the dark nearby. Probably some deer that had just gone on its merry way.

Bastard. I hope you've got internal injuries and you fucking die a painful death.

He put his hands on his hips and sighed again.

If the wheel was fucked, it would be a problem; not an insurmountable one, but a problem nonetheless (unless the axle itself was damaged, but he didn't want to think about that possibility). There was a spare in the boot; he'd just have to move a few things out of the way to get it, including that which had necessitated this journey in the first place. The problem was, it would all take time, and the longer he was stuck here, the more chance of someone – insomniac farmer, bored police patrol – happening across him. And asking awkward questions.

A noise behind made him turn around. What he saw, a few metres away from the rear of the BMW nearly gave him a heart attack. Better that it had done. As it was, he distantly – through his terror, numbing and paralysing – felt both his bladder and bowels evacuate.

And then the thing was on him, tearing and ripping and spilling blood and gobbets of his flesh all over the cold tarmac until he soon knew only blackness, and then nothing.

The impact rudely shocks Brenda from her stupor, though it takes her a few minutes to surface from the black cocoon she is submerged in. In that time, she is aware of – but doesn't really register – the car's suspension shifting as someone exits, a door slamming shut, then muffled footsteps. Finally, there are sounds she wouldn't have been able to make much sense of even if she had been fully cognisant – a strange huffing, a shocked gasp, then wet tearing, crunching, and muffled, phlegmy cries that are soon sharply cut off.

After that, everything goes silent.

When she started coming back to herself, Brenda made to get up – her body felt stuffed with warm cotton wool and she assumed she was in bed or had fallen asleep on the sofa – and subsequently banged her head on the interior of the boot. Not that she knew what it was at first. For a few moments, she simply stared into the darkness in stupefied confusion.

Then, memories returned, flickering images like a kaleidoscope: Gordon, sauntering home two hours late from work yet again, and with no explanation as usual; her tentative queries as to what he'd like for dinner, keeping voice and eyes low so as not to antagonise him too much; his sudden and unexpected eruption of incandescent fury, far beyond anything he'd ever subjected her to, though she'd always suspected him capable of it.

And then… and then…

But it wouldn't come. She had a sense of spiking terror and her heart racing, echoes of his roaring voice and her shocked and high-pitched pleading, but all was without context. However, it didn't take a genius – or all that much of stretch, really, even in her current stupefaction (which was thankfully lifting, though being replaced with a low-grade anxiety that wasn't much better) – to surmise Gordon had attacked or assaulted her.

Brenda snorted without humour. Was there a difference?

She looked around. Picked out as much detail as she could, which wasn't much at all. Even as her eyes adjusted, she still felt she was floating in the depths of space. It was only when she reached out tentatively and her hands touched the interior that she began to suspect where she was.

One thing Brenda Price (née Collins) couldn't be accused of was being slow on the uptake. She'd always excelled at school and college and, even after marrying Gordon, she'd kept her interests in academia and learning going, though she'd intuited early on that Gordon wouldn't approve, so ensured it was never in his face.

Therefore, once the fog began lifting from her thoughts, a number of things became apparent in quick succession.

The first was that, although she had no way of recognising it, she was sure it was the boot of Gordon's BMW she was in (never theirs, always his, even though she contributed towards its upkeep and fuel). The second was that her husband *must* have been the one who placed her here. Third, with her hands and feet untethered, it dawned on her Gordon must either think she was so out of it, she wouldn't wake up...

(*and where is he taking you, hmm? Why are you hidden in the boot and not strapped into a seat as you would be if he were, say, taking you to hospital?* The voice was sly, one she knew of old; her own, but a dark, negative part of her mind that seemed to take joy in her various miseries)

...or, he thought she was dead.

Oh Gordon... Gordon, what have you done?

Bubbling under the chill that suddenly coursed through her body was a rising panic. Stuck in this confined space and feeling the dark *constricting* around her was bringing on a claustrophobia she didn't usually suffer from.

Brenda's breathing sped up in tandem with her heart. Her hands reached out blindly, without control, scrabbling and searching as much as she could in the enclosed space; for what, she didn't know. Burgeoning hysteria just wanted her to move, do something, *anything*. Her nerves screamed.

She made an effort to regulate her breathing.

Calm down, Brenda; just calm the hell down. Think, you fool. Think!

Some sort of collision had woken her, that much she'd worked out already. Then, in the minute or two following that, when she was still fuzzy, there had been other sounds. But when she tried to focus on those, to decipher them, they kept slipping away.

And now all was quiet.

Brenda couldn't hear anything from outside; certainly nothing louder than the heavy beat of her heart or the harsh breaths that kept threatening to turn into rapid gasps. Luckily, the engine had been switched off, otherwise the build-up of fumes might have presented an even worse scenario. But where was her husband and what was he doing? If another vehicle had crashed into them, surely there would be voices outside, arguing or commiserating. Even if it had been caused by some animal, he'd be cursing out loud himself. But there was nothing; the heavy silence ominous and eerie.

Brenda's pulse began to pick up once more; the panic ever-present, waiting to consume her. She took a moment to steady herself again.

Reaching out, this time with more deliberation, Brenda pushed against the inside of the boot's lid. Knowing it would be locked, she still felt disappointment when it didn't budge.

Now what?

She closed her eyes and thought. And it came to her.

Like most modern cars, the rear seats could be flattened down to make more space. If she could just reach the mechanism and release it, she'd be able to put the seats down and wriggle into the main interior of the vehicle. Easier said – or thought – than done, though.

Getting her arms into the right position was, of course, the hardest part. She wasn't a contortionist, didn't even do yoga like most people seemed to these days, which might have helped. However, she was small and slim, and the boot was roomy enough that she could manoeuvre a little. Hopefully enough. Ironic that she had cause to be grateful for Gordon's need for an ego-boosting car, when it was entirely down to him she was here in the first place.

Twisting at the waist, feeling her shoulders stretch to their limits, Brenda managed to get her right arm up against the back of the seats. From there, she used her fingers to creep their way towards the side where the catch was. It wasn't easy, and the further she went, the more pain she caused her overstressed tendons. More than once she had to stop and catch her breath. Who knew such a relatively simple action could be so strenuous? Eventually, she was able to wedge her digits into the tight space between the side of the seat and the car door. Then, it was a matter of slowly moving her fingers around to find the catch, a mechanism that was never designed to be operated from this position. Even when she touched the flat plastic lever, her sweaty fingers slipped twice before she finally gripped it.

She awkwardly pushed the lever and was taken completely by surprise when the seat immediately fell forward and she with it, dumping her upper body into the interior of the car.

She lay sprawled for a moment, gathering breath and thoughts, absently rubbing the strain away from her shoulder. Forty-six and feeling every one of those years. Once she got home (ignoring the voice that whispered *if*), she vowed to partake of more exercise (completely unaware she was echoing her husband's own recent thoughts). She also knew that before *that*, she'd have to deal with Gordon's recent actions, but filed the thought away for later.

Elation filled her, and after returning the back seats to their upright position, she scuttled into the vehicle proper, clambering onto the driver's seat.

A quick check of the ignition showed there were no keys. Typical. The car wasn't a brand-new model and didn't have one of those fancy 'start/stop' buttons. Gordon didn't hold with that kind of innovation; he liked to feel *he* was essential to the starting of the motor, the turning of a key in the ignition somehow granting him this magical power. Same with handbrakes. He didn't like button ones, only those that made that awful ratcheting sound when pulled up. Brenda suspected it was related to absurd notions of 'manliness', though she'd never have voiced this aloud to him.

Just as she was about to get out of the car – wanting little more than to stretch her body, which was now starting to alert her to its myriad aches and bruises, and breathe in some fresh air – she spied her husband, and her hand froze on the door handle.

A few feet beyond the rear of the BMW was Gordon's body.

Brenda was reasonably sure he was dead – a thought that filled her not with horror, regret, or even elation, but with a kind of numb sadness – because he was lying still on the tarmac and his chest was a ruin of torn flesh and exposed organs. The scene was washed in tones of grey monochrome, enough light from the stars and half-moon to give it ghastly detail. Somehow, she thought that was worse than if it had been in full colour.

She stared, grimly fascinated.

What did that? Not the crash; the car would be in a worse state. Some animal? A...a person?

Her thoughts came in a rush, tripping over each other. And with each possible scenario, ramifications followed. If it was an animal, it might well still be out there. Even if it wasn't aware of her presence, there was still plenty of meat on Gordon (the thought of which made her stomach roll in queasiness). Surely a predator wouldn't leave such an abundant food source? And if the perpetrator was human, they would also be out there. The only difference was, an animal wouldn't be able to get in. A person *would*.

Brenda looked out of each window (all closed, thankfully), urgency whipping her head around. Nothing moved outside the car, nothing she could see in the gloom, anyway. The road was deserted, and what little she was able to see of the fields – mostly hidden behind chest-high bushes – looked empty. A killer or beast could be hiding in multiple places and she would never know. Though what animal lay in wait when there was a fresh kill lying in the open?

Without really being aware of it, her mind was pulling towards the notion that some maniac had perpetrated the violence on Gordon. Panic rising yet again, Brenda looked about frantically... and noticed all the little buttons on the doors were up, indicating they were unlocked. She scrabbled around for the central locking switch. Found it, pushed it. Nothing. Of course; the engine was off.

Crap. What to do? What to do?

Brenda contemplated jumping outside to grab the keys. Worry that she would freeze upon being that close to Gordon's dead body, that whatever had killed him – *mutilated, eviscerated*, whispered that treacherous part of her mind – was waiting for her to do just that, made her hesitate.

She was in danger of being paralysed by indecision. *Some* kind of action had to be taken. Kneeling on the seat, Brenda raised herself as far as she could to try and look out over the bushes and the fields behind them. In the dark, there was little to see. The limits of her vision ended perhaps a couple of dozen metres beyond the edge of the fields, the grey land fading into a deep black. She shifted around, peering out of each window in turn with much the same result. And still no sign of whatever had ripped Gordon to bits.

Just as she was about to give in to the hopelessness that threatened to engulf her – bitter tears prickled the corners of her eyes and a sharp lump sat in her throat – she spotted something away in the distance, a tiny pinprick of light that at first she thought she was imagining, called into being by her desperation. Brenda pressed her forehead against the cold glass of the car's windscreen. No, there was definitely something there. Further down the road – the car had come to a halt at the top of a slight rise, the road leading gently downhill before it – and a little off to the left were tiny, flickering lights. Maybe they were just low hanging stars, but Brenda didn't think so; they were too yellow and just a shade too large. They *had* to be lights shining in the windows of some building. Maybe a farmhouse or solitary cottage. If she could get there, they'd have a phone she could use.

Again, she thought of creeping out of the vehicle and retrieving the keys. Again, the idea of being attacked made her waver.

But she couldn't sit here all night. Or could she? Maybe inaction was the best plan. Someone was bound to come along eventually. Unless that someone was the maniac who'd torn Gordon to pieces. And since she couldn't lock the doors without the keys, she was vulnerable to a human attacker.

But that idea didn't sit well with Brenda, and not only because of the growing suspicion some crazy person was out there. She'd spent most of her life with Gordon – everything before then had all but faded anyway, some remote dream she'd once had – in meek passivity, and the thought of continuing like that, even just for one night when it might make the most sense, made her brain itch. No more. She had to start taking control of her life and it had to start now.

Just as she was about to open the driver's door to get the keys – not caring if the decision proved to be a reckless one, only sure she had to act with purpose – movement caught on the periphery of her vision, and for the second time that night she paused while carrying out the same action.

What she saw scattered all thoughts of exiting the safety of the car like so much paper shredded and blown before a gale.

At least now she had the answer of whether it was

animal or man that had obliterated Gordon. (Though in the back of her numb mind, that hateful voice had slipped from sly condescension into screaming hysteria, a high-pitched but thankfully – for now – faint cry of, *it's a monster, it's a monster!*)

Outlined in pale moonlight, the... *thing* – Brenda couldn't say what it was, but it was definitely *not* human – slunk almost casually around Gordon's body, occasionally nudging his dead flesh with its snout. The body was long and thick, tubular, dipping slightly in the middle. It was also huge; easily the size of an adult tiger, perhaps even bigger. The legs had something of the reptile about them, but were long and muscular with large splayed feet. And the head... Well, that was the most terrifying thing of all. Even though it was dark and the creature's colouring matched the greys of the environment (Brenda distantly wondered if it was indeed the same washed out shades as those around it; it certainly blended well with the backdrop – it could have been lying on the grass verge all this time and she wouldn't have noticed), she was able to pick out the detail of the head quite clearly. She'd never seen anything like it, and she loved watching wildlife shows. In contrast to the soft-looking trunk, the skull was all sharp angles and knobs and ridges. In fact, it was as though the bones were on the *outside* of the head, giving it a frightening mask-like appearance. She couldn't guess its species; there was something of the crocodile there, but the snout was too wide and thick. It could equally be related to a dog or large cat. Absurdly, what it *most* reminded her of was those traditional costumes worn by Chinese people. The

Lion Dance, she thought it might have been called. Brightly coloured, beautifully decorated two- or three-person outfits, they were supposed to represent the beast the performance was named for, but to Brenda, they had always seemed more like dragons. And despite the gaudiness of them, they had terrified her. Now this thing was here and it looked like the real-life monster the costumes were based on, but with none of the charm or vibrancy. It even had a thick mane of short hair, though the rest of the body appeared hairless.

It was very obviously a predator, and very obviously responsible for reducing Gordon to a pile of shredded meat.

Her heart hammering, her nerves screaming, Brenda slowly hunkered down on the driver's seat, hoping to minimise her profile. She didn't think the thing had seen her; it looked to be fully occupied with Gordon's corpse. It nosed the body one last time then opened its jaws – *oh my God, look at the size of that mouth! And those teeth!* – and clamped them on Gordon's left shoulder. Brenda saw tendons strain and tighten, then heard the crunch as its teeth bit through flesh and bone in one movement. It raised its head and worked its mouth as it chewed and swallowed. As grim as the scene was, Brenda found she couldn't look away. What was it? Some new species? It seemed to be composed of numerous animals, but resembled none. Surely nothing like this could have remained hidden in the UK. Though now she thought about it, there *were* all those reports of supposed big cats running amok in the country. The Beast of Bodmin Moor and all that, wild animals no-one could ever get a decent picture or sighting of. Absently, in numb shock, Brenda shook her head; no, those stories were just that. As made-up as the Loch Ness Monster.

Her musings were cut short when the creature paused its feeding and turned sharply to look at the car. Brenda stopped breathing. Had it seen her move?

Idiot.

She chastised herself, even as her skin prickled and her blood ran with rippling chills.

The thing lifted its head higher, the neck stretching. It was definitely looking at the car.

After a moment, it padded slowly over, in no hurry. And why would it be, she thought. Lying on the road was a ready source of food, and inside the vehicle another potential meal. Brenda shuddered at the thought, tremors coursing from the top of her head all the way down to her feet, into her very bones.

She watched as the monster moved up alongside the vehicle, slipping silently past the driver's side. She realised she was still holding her breath and tried to take in little sips of air as quietly as she could. It seemed to take an age to go past, and she was reminded of the movie *Jaws*, the way the shark would glide like a ghost past ships and boats. That thought caused a cascade of images from movies featuring wild animals attacking humans, scary films she hadn't realised at the time were actually horrors. She looked down to see her hands trembling and understood she was on the verge of losing it, panic seconds away from overtaking her.

Though it took a massive effort, Brenda closed her eyes and concentrated on her breathing. Slowly, she brought it back down, though it was still ragged and hitching. Her pulse she could do little about, but at least the maelstrom swirl of her thoughts had calmed somewhat.

She opened her eyes and looked around but could no longer see the beast.

Crap. Think, Brenda, think. It's an animal – a weird looking one at that, but still an animal. It can't open doors, so you're safe as long as you don't go outside.

She almost giggled at the thought of simply opening the door and stepping casually outside to her doom. Her brief prison was now her refuge. How ironic.

And it doesn't matter how fearsome it looks, I doubt it can just smash its way through the windows.

That last she wasn't entirely confident of.

She glanced quickly outside, but there was no sign of it. Perhaps it wasn't aware of her after all and had simply wandered off. It was a lovely thought, though one she couldn't indulge in too much. And sure enough, no sooner had she thought it than the beast appeared, this time on the passenger side.

It rose up to place its feet on the window, and Brenda almost let out a scream when she caught the motion in her peripheral vision and heard the dull thud against glass. The car rocked, a lazy sway, and Brenda was acutely aware of the strength behind the push. Perhaps it was fully capable of smashing through after all.

It turned its head one way then the other, and she realised it was searching the interior. The eyes were set back in that skull-like head, little points of glistening light in deep caverns. Yet she swore she could sense a level of intelligence there that went beyond mere animal cunning. It could simply have been her fear superimposing something that wasn't there, but the fact was, this thing didn't behave like other animals; it moved with calculated deliberation, without the instinctual behaviour she'd expect in a predator. It was deeply unnerving to her.

Brenda shrunk back against the car door's interior, the handle digging into her back. She barely noticed. The beast had stopped craning its head and was now peering at her with one beady little eye. It pushed against the window, as though testing the strength of the glass, and the car moved again. She had the impression it could tip the vehicle completely over if it wanted to. Its claws – black and sharp and *big* – cut lines in the window as the creature slowly contracted them, the movement accompanied by a nerve-shredding screech.

And then it dropped down and disappeared.

So unexpected was this, Brenda was taken aback and sat where she was in dumb stupefaction. But soon enough, her wits came back and with them, her fear.

Where was it? What on earth was it doing? She had to know.

Heart pounding, Brenda rose up on her knees and looked once again out through the windows. Nothing. It was nowhere to be seen. She wasn't sure if this was worse. If it weren't for the utterly alien and terrifying appearance of it, she might have said it was better to be able to keep an eye on it.

Stretching up, she took another look out, making sure to check the shadows of the grass verge and the bushes. No sign.

Sitting back down, Brenda chewed her lip.

Waiting didn't seem to be any kind of option at all. Even if it couldn't get in the car – and she was beginning to think it was only a matter of time before the creature decided to just jump through a window – she would go insane waiting on someone else to happen by. And what would happen then? That poor bastard would get out, thinking they were helping someone, and then the monster would tear *them* to bits, too. No... she had to do something, but what?

Her thoughts snagged again on the faint light she'd seen further down the road. It had to be a house, just *had* to. But how to get to them? And then it slowly came to her; it was thinking of the word 'down' that did it.

As she'd previously noted, the car was on the crest of a low hill. If she released the handbrake, it should – in theory – start rolling down the slope, towards where the lights were. She might have to give it a little encouragement – rock it back and forth – but surely gravity would be her friend.

There was no point in procrastinating.

Offering up a little prayer to Gordon's otherwise hitherto annoying machismo, Brenda grabbed the handbrake and pushed it down.

The car didn't move.

Well, you knew it might not be that easy.

She settled in behind the steering wheel, crossed herself, then began rocking back and forth. Still nothing. Trying to keep a lid on her panic, Brenda increased the rhythm of her movements, aware of how ludicrous she must look, but not caring.

Come on... Come on, you bastard! Move!

Biting down on a scream, she slapped the steering wheel. Tears of frustration stung her eyes; bitter disappointment burned the back of her throat.

Brenda lifted her head to the dark sky. Why? Why was this happening to her? First, Gordon exploding at nothing, then whatever he'd done to her to render her unconscious. Bundling her unconscious form into the boot of the BMW to... what? Dispose of her body? And finally, being stranded in the car and stalked by some creature from the darkest of nightmares.

Lord, what have I done to deserve this? Was I evil in a past life? God, please, please help me.

But even as she thought that, she felt guilt and shame. Her mother had instilled in her that to be human was to suffer and one must be humble and grateful for it. God only helped those who helped themselves and begging for His assistance was unseemly and egotistical. Prideful. Entreating God to solve one's difficulties was a sin, one of many in a long, long list of sins according to Ma Collins. Though she'd slipped away from the shadow of her mother many years previously (albeit into the equally smothering embrace of Gordon), the woman's influence still clung.

Hot on the heels of those thoughts, though, was the eternal argument that if God were as all powerful as His worshippers made out, then He was the one responsible for all this in the first place. But her mother would have had a ready answer to that as well.

"God is always testing us, Brenda. We must never be complacent or forget we only exist through his infinite mercy and tolerance, and He must be sure we are worthy of His love

and salvation. He tests us, and it is up to us to show we are capable of rising to those challenges without complaint."

Though the 'lesson' didn't work quite the way her mother had intended – attempts at hardening Brenda to the harsh world her mother saw beyond their household had, instead, made the girl, then woman, more fearful and nervous – it still gave her something to cling to, now. Her breathing slowed, the panic abated, and her thoughts slowly settled.

And then before she could think of what to do next, the thing jumped up against the window next to her.

Brenda shrieked – a short, sharp exclamation of surprise – and scuttled over to the passenger side, the handbrake digging into her backside as she went, though she barely noticed. She fetched up against the passenger door, her back pressed into its uncomfortable surface. Her heart raced and her breathing came in ragged pants. Jesus, but she couldn't take much more of this.

The creature stared in at her. The whole car had shifted again beneath its weight and power, yet even in her shock she had the suspicion it wasn't using half the strength it could.

It eyed her for another few seconds then dropped down out of sight.

Almost immediately, it reappeared at the passenger door window, jumping up again and causing the vehicle to shift violently once more.

What the hell? Is it playing with me?

Something about its actions reminded her of a cat, toying with prey or a stuffed animal. What the hell was this thing?

She could worry about that later, if there was one. Right now, the association had sparked inspiration.

Keeping her gaze on the creature – as it kept its gaze on her – Brenda slowly clambered into the rear of the car. It followed her movements, that big skull head angling towards her. Once she was kneeling on the rear seats, it dropped down again and jumped up against the rear window on the passenger side. It *was* playing with her, whatever play meant to this beast. Regardless, it wasn't displaying the behaviours she'd normally associate with a wild predator, none of the crazed bloodlust she'd witnessed on those wildlife documentaries.

She hoped what she had planned worked.

Very gently, keeping one leg on the car seat, Brenda slid her body onto the parcel shelf beneath the BMW's rear window. She rested one arm on the back of the seats, fearing even her slight weight might collapse the thin material. When she was in place, she reached out and slapped the back window.

The creature stared at her, its mouth slightly open. Brenda could see the tongue in there, a thick slab of dark meat, squirming and moving. It made her feel queasy.

Just as she thought it wasn't going to do what she wanted – *needed* – it to do, it left its position and came around to the rear of the car.

And simply stood there looking at her.

"Come on, you freak. Jump. Jump up. Why can't you do this one thing for me?"

She kept slapping the palm of her hand against the glass, and the creature just kept staring at her.

"Oh, for crying out loud, why can't something go right for me just for *once*?"

Then it *did* move. Crouching back on its haunches and opening its mouth to let out a low moan (Brenda realised it was the first time she'd heard the thing make a noise, and it was both unlike what she might have thought it would be and deeply unsettling; a low exhalation, almost like a weary sigh), it launched itself at the back of the car.

The impact pushed the car forward and Brenda fell against the backs of the front seats. Her breath came out in a whoosh. Then the car was rolling. It was actually moving. She almost couldn't believe it and lay where she was in stunned surprise.

Then it occurred to her that without someone guiding the car, it would likely smash up against a tree or land in a ditch.

Scrabbling, Brenda pulled herself up and climbed into the driver's seat again. She risked a glance behind and was puzzled to see the creature where it had been when it pushed the car. Perhaps it was confused as to what had happened. Whatever, she couldn't spare much thought for it right then.

She faced the road ahead and grabbed the steering wheel.

Though the slope of the road was relatively shallow, the heavy car was picking up speed; not too fast, but fast enough considering the engine was off and the controls were limited. She pumped the brakes. They caught a little, but weren't as firm as they should be. Oh well. She'd just have to use the handbrake as well, and hope to hell it stopped the thing before she had an accident. The way her luck was going tonight, she'd end up getting seriously injured in a car crash.

Brenda held on tight to the steering wheel, mostly to stop the BMW veering off into a field, correcting its course as it trundled down the road, though the mechanism was stiff, the wheel near enough locked into position.

Off to the left, the lights she'd spotted grew closer and closer. She could see now it was definitely a house, a sprawling bungalow approaching very quickly. Another thirty seconds or so and she'd be outside the short driveway.

A quick check of the rear-view mirror showed the beast still at the top of the road. What on earth was it waiting for? She wondered if perhaps it didn't want to leave Gordon's body, a source of food that was guaranteed, to go chasing off after an unknown quantity. It didn't matter; all it did was afford her time to get from the car to the house. She only hoped the lights being on meant someone was in.

Then she was there. Brenda stomped on the footbrake. The car juddered, she felt it slow, but it didn't stop. Panicking, she kept pumping the pedal, and at the same time yanked the handbrake up (ignoring that awful ratcheting sound Gordon loved). The car juddered and even though it wasn't going that fast, the tyres still skidded across the tarmac surface. It came to a rude stop and Brenda was thrown forward, her shoulders hitting the steering wheel. Any faster and it would have caused some real damage. As it was, she was dazed for only a moment.

Didn't even think to put on the seatbelt. Stupid.

She shook her head and got out of the car, stifling a snigger at the thought of the safety admonishment.

A quick look up the road chilled her blood. The beast was nowhere to be seen.

Crap!

She scrabbled round the front of the car and along the short driveway. Stones crunched beneath her shoes. When she reached the door, she started banging on it, fists pounding weakly.

"Help, help. Please, someone, help. Oh, *please* be awake."

She almost didn't hear the footsteps approach from the other side over her own noise.

When the front door opened, Brenda half fell in, one arm raised in the act of knocking. A half-seen figure stepped to one side and a voice exclaimed, "Oh my..."

Brenda took a few steps into the brightly lit hall, her eyes blinking in the unaccustomed light. She turned to see a small, grey-haired old man in at least his sixties, staring at her with confusion pasted across his face.

"Quick, close the door! We're not safe, you need to secure the house. Please, hurry!" She tried to keep her voice from rising to a scream, but she couldn't stop the volume from going up on her last few words.

Yet the man did as she said, though slowly, oh so slowly, so that Brenda wanted to tear her hair out, wanted to roar, wanted to push him out of the way and slam it closed herself.

Finally, the door was shut, and Brenda nearly collapsed in the hallway. As it was, she did sink to her knees, her legs suddenly losing what strength had carried her this far. Now the danger was mitigated a little – if not entirely gone, which would be infinitely better – she was coming to realise just how great a toll stress, fear, and panic had wrought on her. Luckily, there was another person there to steady her as she slipped downwards.

Warm arms wrapped in a scratchy cardigan enfolded her, and a voice spoke above and over her head.

"There, now. I've got you. Don't worry, you're okay, hen. Harold, give me a hand. Let's get the poor lassie into the sitting-room. She's obviously crashed her car or something. Needs a cup of tea."

The man – Harold – must have obeyed immediately as another pair of hands came from behind to support her elbows as they both lifted her up.

A cup of tea. Sounds wonderful. And then maybe a little nap...

But before she lost herself in thoughts of blessed oblivion, she remembered what had brought her here.

Almost rudely, Brenda pulled herself out of the arms of her would-be saviours.

"No. No! There's no time for that. Where's your phone? I need to call the police."

Both of them looked at her in wary confusion, near-identical kindly old wrinkled faces scrunched up in affront and mild shock.

"I'm sorry, I don't mean to sound like a crazy woman—" which was, she realised, *exactly* how she sounded "—but I have to call the police, the army, someone. Please... where is your phone?" Brenda held up her hands in supplication.

The woman gestured to the left. "It's just there, beside the kitchen door, on the other side. But is...is everything okay? Why don't you sit down for a minute and tell us what's happened."

Brenda shook her head. "I can't. We don't have much time."

The old woman clutched the top of her cardigan and Harold simply gaped.

Brenda turned away and found the phone inside the kitchen. She dialled nine-nine-nine then waited with excruciating impatience as it rang out. Eventually she was put through to an operator and from there to the police. The controller asked in a bored voice what her emergency was.

"Listen, you need to send someone with guns, someone in animal control, anyone! There's some... creature out here and it killed my husband and it tried to get me—" She knew this was a slight exaggeration, but still... "—and who knows who else it's attacked."

"Okay, ma'am, if you could just take a breath and tell me what kind of animal it is and where you are?"

"I don't know what it is, it's not anything I've ever seen before, but it's huge and weird and it's aggressive and it's killed! Do you not understand that?"

There was a sigh on the other end. Brenda couldn't believe it. *"Ma'am, we need to know what kind of animal we're dealing with so we can send the right people with the right—"* There was a buzz and the voice clicked off mid-sentence.

Brenda frowned at the handset for a moment. "What?"

She pushed down on the switch and dialled again.

This time, all she got was the engaged tone. Tried again and again with the same result.

Slowly, she hung up, a thin thread of cold terror snaking through her guts. She turned around to see the old couple had gotten closer. "Your phone... it doesn't seem to be working." The words were spoken in a daze. Something about the situation had really spooked her, and that was saying something, considering what she'd already gone through tonight.

The woman was looking at her with an odd expression on her face. "Did you say... some kind of animal was *attacking* people?"

Brenda nodded, barely listening. Her mind was racing down half-formed paths. "Do either of you have a mobile I could use? Please... it's vital we inform the authorities."

The couple exchanged a look. Then the woman came forward. "Listen, dear. Why don't you sit down and we'll see if we can't sort this all out, eh? Come through to the sitting-room. I'll get the brews on. Everything's always better after a cuppa, aye?"

With that, the old woman guided Brenda towards a door back in the hall. She opened it and ushered Brenda ahead, speaking all the while, and over Brenda's weak protests. "I'm Sadie, hen. Sarah, that is, but everyone calls me Sadie. What would you like? Tea, coffee, something stronger?"

Before she could wonder why the room beyond the door was shrouded in darkness, Brenda felt a surprisingly firm push against her back and fell forward.

And kept falling, as it turned out there was a staircase beyond the doorway. She tumbled down a half-dozen steps and came to rest in a heap at the bottom, sprawled on a cold, close-packed dirt floor. Above, Sadie called down, "Sorry, dear, but I think you must have met Errol, and we can't have you alerting the authorities to him."

The door above was quickly shut and Brenda heard the sound of a key being turned.

She sat up, setting off a myriad of aches. A quick check suggested nothing was seriously damaged, only bruises and a couple of small cuts. Thankfully, it was only a few steps down to... where was she anyway? Brenda looked around. Though this space wasn't as brightly lit as the main house, there was enough ambient light to see it was, essentially, a cellar-type room, though of course it wasn't all that much lower than the house proper. Perhaps the cottage was some kind of converted farmhouse, and this used to be a stable or barn. Regardless, it was bare and unfurnished, not a room for habitation. At least not by humans. There was a tart smell in the air, a sharp, unpleasant tang that Brenda associated with zoos and safari parks; it hit the back of her throat and made her eyes water. Coupled with the pile of bones to her right – tucked just to one side of the staircase and looking mostly like small animal bones, thankfully – and the big hole leading under the far wall, she was beginning to get a very bad feeling about this place.

Brenda marched up the steps and banged on the door. "Open this right now! How dare you lock me down here. What do you think you're doing?"

There was no answer at first.

She knocked again, the door trembling under her assault. "Come on, then! Let me out of here. Now!"

She heard shuffling steps on the other side.

Then; "I'm sorry, dear, but we can't have them finding out about Errol and taking him away or hurting him. You see, we found him as a wee baby, and we've been looking after him for months, now. He's really not as bad as you think. If he hurt your husband, I don't doubt it was a mistake. He probably scared Errol, or attacked him. The wee mite would only have been defending himself. He's actually quite affectionate when you know him. Intelligent, too."

What on earth is this woman babbling about? She sounds nuts. 'Affectionate'? 'A mistake'? Has she seen this thing in action? Errol? They're off their trollies.

Brenda stepped back, stumbling down the stairs onto the ground. She staggered, feeling woozy. This nightmare just didn't seem like it was going to end anytime soon. That made her think. Maybe this *was* just a nightmare, maybe she was still lying in the trunk of the BMW unconscious and dreaming. Or better yet, asleep at home in her comfy bed.

No. That way lay madness. She couldn't afford the false comfort thinking like that brought. She'd was here and had to deal with it. She'd slept her way through life with Gordon and enough was enough.

Raising her voice, Brenda called out in as calm a voice as she could muster, "Sadie, I need you to listen to me very carefully; 'Errol', as you call it, is not some lost puppy or harmless little animal. He – *it* – is wild and dangerous. It needs to be handled by the proper authorities. You have to believe me."

There was some rapid whispering she couldn't decipher, then; "Sorry, love, we're just too attached to him. But you'll see; he'll be home any minute, now. I'm sure you'll see the gentle side of him that we have."

Brenda's pulse spiked, her heart beating painfully. "Sadie, listen! My name is Brenda Price, and—"

"No, no, no, we don't need to hear that. We're off to make some tea, now. We'll chat later."

Despite her screams for them to come back, to let her out, Brenda heard them shuffle away from the door, then heard another door close.

She was on her own.

'...he'll be home any minute.'

It was as she'd suspected; this room was Errol's living space. She had to get out. But how?

The only way, other than the door that was securely locked, was the hole across the room. A hole she guessed had either been dug by Errol or had been made for it by his stupid, naïve, adopted 'owners'. A hole the creature clearly used to get out and hunt. To kill. Perhaps it had only been doing this recently; otherwise, Brenda was sure she'd have heard something on the news. Surely such a creature couldn't go unnoticed. Nor would a spate of disappearances or mutilated bodies. Sadie and Harold must have been feeding it small animals if the pile of little bones was anything to go by. But now it had gotten out and had tasted human flesh.

Brenda shook herself. All this idle musing was a waste of time, She had to go, immediately.

She scampered over to the hole, prepared to dive right in and hopefully to some kind of freedom – though fully aware Errol was still out there – when the sound of dirt shifting came from the other side.

Oh... crap.

She took a step back, then another as the sounds grew louder. By the time she'd moved back to the other side of the room, her heels bumping against the bottom step, Errol was pushing his way in.

The beast slithered in like a snake or lizard. Jesus, but it seemed to emulate so many animals without resembling fully any.

It was immediately aware of her presence, the head swivelling in her direction. Its little eyes – those bright pinpricks that resembled the shining stars in the night sky – regarded her with alien intention, though she reckoned she could take an educated guess at what it was thinking. Her legs wobbled with fear-induced weakness, and she stumbled back, tripping on the stairs and depositing her backside on them with a thump.

Errol came closer, a few measured, deliberate steps. No-one was coming to save her; there were no last-minute reprieves in life. It was simply another example of the cruelty and harshness of the universe, just as her mother had warned. But instead of deriving meagre comfort from belief in God as Ma Collins had, Brenda was overwhelmed by the sheer random savagery of existence, by the idea that God allowed such awful things to happen to His creations. It simply made little sense to her, filled her with a bone-deep grief.

Another step, one massive paw kicking up a puff of dirt from the ground.

Brenda felt pressure in her abdomen and held on, not wanting the indignity of wetting herself in her final moments. She wouldn't give this thing the satisfaction.

Her hands reached out either side to steady herself, scrabbling blindly in the dirt. As if from a distance, she was aware of her right hand slipping into the pile of bones at her side.

A few more steps and Errol was close enough that she could reach out and touch it, if she were so inclined. She was also able to smell its breath, a fetid, dank stench that made her want to vomit. It forced her to take sips of air through her mouth, though she fancied she could still taste the foulness. She even thought she could feel heat emanating from its body, pulsing at her in waves.

It opened its mouth and flicked its thick tongue out, as if testing the air or tasting her smell. Brenda cringed away from its attentions, slipping off the steps and onto the ground. She tried to push herself through the wall behind; if only it were that easy. Her back merely scraped painfully against the bare concrete. Seemingly of its own accord, her right hand foraged through the bones of small animals until her fingers found one that was long and sharp at one end. All of a sudden, anger bloomed in her mind, eclipsing the terror and revulsion that had been driving her actions. All her frustrations and sense of unfairness and a rage that had been growing within her for years and years coalesced into a pinpoint white heat. How unfair it all was, how absolutely dismaying to have lived through everything she had only to come to this sad end. Well, she wouldn't go without some kind of fight.

The beast dipped its head closer, a rumbling sigh escaping its mouth. Brenda gripped the shard of bone in a tight fist and swung with the force of pent-up fury.

Though the sharp end plunged into Errol's neck below the jaw, in her mind Brenda was stabbing Gordon, retribution for years of mental torture and verbal abuse.

She screamed as she stabbed, a primal yell of savage vengeance. "Leave. Me. The fuck. Alone!" It might well have been the first time she'd cursed in about twenty-five years.

The beast bellowed, spraying her face with warm breath and saliva. But it backed away, the piece of bone still lodged in its neck. A thin trickle of blood leaked out from where the shard penetrated.

Looking quickly down, Brenda found another piece of bone and held it up in front of her. If Errol came at her again, she'd stick this one in it, too. Yet the creature didn't seem keen. It put distance between them before sitting down on its haunches and trying to claw the bone out. However, its paw wasn't dextrous enough to do so. It only seemed to be causing itself more pain, whimpering every time a claw touched the bone fragment. Perhaps this was the first time it had ever been attacked or injured.

A clamour at the door made her look around. It opened and the old couple spilled in, Harold holding a kitchen knife in one trembling hand. He brandished it at her weakly, but as soon as they spotted Errol sitting in pain, they both rushed over. Brenda noted with satisfaction they kept a little distance between themselves and the creature.

Sadie dropped to her knees a couple of feet in front of her 'pet'. "Errol, oh Errol... What has that bitch done to you? My poor wee boy."

'Bitch'? That's a bit much. Stupid cow.

Harold turned around and made what he probably thought was a threatening gesture with the knife. "You just stay there. We'll deal with you in a minute." He turned back to the monster.

Brenda had no intention of obeying. She staggered to her feet, her legs shaking. Christ, but this night was taking its toll. She *definitely* needed to start hitting the gym. She almost giggled at the idea of improved physical fitness being the biggest lesson of the events of this night, and recognised that reaction as burgeoning hysteria. She bit down on it.

The old couple still had their attentions on Errol. Brenda started up the steps, taking each one slowly and carefully, keeping all three in her sights. Before she could exit the room, however, Errol decided it was time for its comeback.

Harold had leaned in closer than his wife, and was reaching out tentatively towards the beast. Maybe he was as stressed as Brenda, or perhaps he had some kind of dementia, but it seemed he had forgotten he was holding the knife in the hand he was extending. And Errol apparently didn't like that. Perhaps it thought Harold was going to attack. Twisting its head, the beast clamped its jaws on Harold's forearm and bit down. There was the horrible sound of bone crunching and Harold's arm dropped to the ground in a spray of blood. The man stared dumbly at it for a second, then opened his mouth and released a steadily rising scream as blood pulsed from the severed stump. He fell back onto his rear, holding the ruin of his arm aloft and continuing to scream.

Meanwhile, Sadie had stood up, and was now wagging a finger at Errol. Brenda couldn't believe what she was seeing. The woman had just watched her husband receive an amputation from this nightmare creature and she was scolding it! These two definitely had more than a few screws loose.

"Bad Errol, naughty boy. That wasn't very nice, now, was it?"

And the thing was looking up at her as if listening, as if it knew what she was saying.

Brenda decided it was time to leave, to get out of this madhouse.

She slipped out of the room and into the hallway, heading for the door.

And was subsequently thrown back against one wall as the front door exploded in a shower of splinters.

Shadowy figures poured in through the entrance, flooding past her. One grabbed her and pressed her into the wall. In her shock, she saw they were all wearing the same kind of uniform – black overalls and armour, with guns held in their arms and attached to their person. Relief drenched her. It was the military or the police. She was saved. There *was* such a thing as a last-second rescue after all.

Even though the officer had her wrists held together in a tight grip, and was pushing her uncomfortably against the wall, Brenda felt gratitude. Everything would be all right, now. She was saved.

She felt like she'd been in the cell for days, though it couldn't have been more than a few hours at most.

Brenda tapped her fingers on the steel table she was sitting behind. At least she hadn't been handcuffed, though the surface had a thick steel ring welded to it that she assumed was for just that purpose. The room was square and small, grey and oppressive. A place to hold prisoners.

Finally, the door opened and a man walked in. Brenda caught a glimpse of a black-clad figure outside, standing to attention like a guard. Her visitor was dressed differently. He wore a neatly pressed uniform with a number of medal ribbons on the left breast, though there were no insignia she recognised.

He stood in front of her, on the other side of the table.

His face was craggy and hard, as if chiselled from stone. His dark eyes were both flat and piercing and his grey hair was cut close to his skull. She knew he was someone in charge, and his mere presence filled her with dread.

He folded his arms. "So, Mrs Price. Have you had a chance to think about your situation?"

She chewed her lip but remained silent.

He continued. "You've had a very long night and been through events few people could contemplate. It's understandable that your perception might not be at its most... reliable. It's easy to mistake things under extreme circumstances. I see it all the time in soldiers. And you're not one of those. You understand?"

Brenda met his gaze even though she wanted to look away. She nodded slowly. "Listen... I don't care what line you give the public, what story you want me to stick to. I've got no interest in mouthing off. Just tell me...just tell me you've gotten rid of that...that *thing*. Tell me it's been taken care of, that it's been destroyed. That's all I care about."

The man regarded her for a time that seemed to stretch longer than it was. Just when she thought she couldn't bear it anymore – when she thought she might scream just to break the silence – he spoke. "You don't need to worry about that ever again. You have my word. It's been completely taken care of."

Brenda's whole body sagged. She hadn't even been aware of how rigid she'd been holding herself. "Then I accept whatever you want me to accept. I'll stick to whatever you tell me to."

She nodded, mostly to herself. As long as that monster was dead, she could keep silent about what had really happened tonight. No sense in being labelled a nutter by the public or incurring the wrath of the military. Never mind that they were essentially gaslighting her, just as Gordon had done for most of their married life. It was a burden she could bear with ease. She was free, now; free to live the rest of her life as she wished, not in fear of her husband and not in fear of any nightmare creature. It was time to start finding out just who she really was.

Brenda released a long sigh and smiled to herself.

Major William Donlan walked down one of many corridors in the secret facility located beneath the Greenmarsh army base. At his side was Alistair McCracken, one of a number of scientists attached to the project Donlan was overseeing. The white-jacketed civilian had to keep adjusting his walk with little hops to keep up with Donlan's long strides.

McCracken looked up at his taller companion as they walked. "Do you really think the woman will keep quiet?"

Donlan didn't pause or glance at McCracken. "I do. The compensation she'll receive should be more than enough incentive. And even if she doesn't, who will believe her? But we'll keep an eye on her at any rate. If she blabs, it won't be much of an effort to have her disappeared. She has no family, after all; no-one who might miss her. But I suspect she'll stay silent. All she needed to believe was that the 'creature' was dead."

McCracken nodded. "Understandable."

They halted outside a metal door, a thick slab with a panel set in it at average head height. For the first time, Donlan looked at the scientist. "And how is our... wayward child?"

McCracken looked down at the tablet he was carrying. "Well, we're still trying to work out how it got out in the first place. It must have crawled out through a vent or pipe when it was smaller, perhaps whilst on transit to the testing facility. But it seems relatively stable, aside from clearly developing a taste for human flesh. But... that could be construed as an advantage..."

"Indeed." Donlan slowly slid open the hatch on the door. Within, something large and heavy shuffled and a low growl drifted through the opening. "They grow up so fast..." His voice was low, almost contemplative.

Eventually, Donlan slammed shut the hatch and stepped back. "Might be we'll be moving onto the next phase quicker than we thought."

They both looked down the long corridor, which had dozens of identical doors on both sides, just like the one they were standing in front of. The corridor stretched off into the distance. And from behind those doors came a variety of sounds; growls, cries, the occasional roar or hiss, yelps and screeches.

Donlan nodded. "Yes... things are progressing *very* well. Soon, we'll be ready."

With a final glance at the locked door, Donlan spun on his heel and walked off, McCracken trailing in his wake.

The Goddess of the Rain
Alison Littlewood

It was a stark and formless light; that was all I could see the first time I glanced at her, and all I could make out for some seconds afterwards, as if I had been temporarily blinded by lightning. That was how I felt too – as if I'd been struck. Even then, I was left with the faint scent of phosphorous in my nostrils, as if a match had ignited or I'd just escaped a fire.

Dance music pounded in my ears and the club's crowd sighed in unison, the whole swarmy might of them pulsing and shifting with the rhythm. And I caught a sudden sight of her again – her gleaming skin catching the flare of a spotlight, the diaphanous crimson dress clinging to her form, the shine of her eyes.

I had to be with her and couldn't reach her, even then, but I knew I had to try. So I ducked and weaved, catching brief glimpses: a lurid flare limning her features, hair that was part cornrows, part loose tangles whipping about her head. I saw her in fragments, as if I could only take her in a little at a time and anything else might be too much.

Then I was in front of her, and as if she'd been expecting me I felt the pressure of her hands on my shoulders, running down my back, making the hair stand up along my arms, making me shiver.

She smiled. Her teeth flashed. Her eyes held depths within them, like peering through layers of deep water. I wanted to ask her a thousand things – who she was, where she came from, why I hadn't seen her before, would she marry me, those kinds of things – but somehow no words came. After a moment I reached for her, catching a trail of that gauzy dress. I danced with her, admired her, *worshipped* her, until it felt like we had reached a place almost without words, where not even our names remained to us; where we didn't want them and didn't care, because we no longer needed them.

The crowds began to thin as the club emptied. I didn't notice time passing until she caught me by the hand and led me outside, into a world that clamoured with rain and groaned with thunder. We were drenched at once and I began to make some banal comment about it – terrible weather, so unexpected, could I lend her my coat, could I *give* it to her, or anything I had?

She put a finger to my lips, whirling away from me, laughing, holding out her arms to receive the rain. Shining droplets shone in her hair, her dress clinging ever more tightly to her breasts, her hips, the curve of her back. I wanted her more than I'd ever wanted anything and I reached for her, bringing her lips to mine. What I felt was like the tingling jolt of an electric shock but I didn't stop, only holding her closer, as if I could protect her with my body – as if the heat between us could keep her warm.

She put her lips to my ear and whispered, "I brought the rain for you."

Her accent was impossible to place, but it was beautiful and I kissed her again. And again she took me by the hand, leading me away with not a thought for the water that splashed to our ankles or dripped down our necks or drenched our clothes and hair.

It was a spark of dawn's first light that woke me, penetrating the window in the anodyne hotel room, showing me the patterned carpet and the wooden desk with its notices about breakfast and check-out times and Wi-Fi. Distantly, a door banged; a television rumbled; rain steadily spattered the window. All of it whispered to me that she would already be gone, but when I turned she was there: eyes closed, hair spread on the pillow, her smooth shoulder jutting from the sheets. A memory rose of touching that skin and suddenly I couldn't breathe. It had never been like that for me before and I couldn't imagine it ever being that way again; I wished I could wrap myself around her and never leave this room. Even the rain was welcome, the sound hemming us in, holding us in thrall. All night the storm had raged, turning everything into a glory of light that had somehow fitted; our every movement, every breath had been echoed in the pulsing of the sky outside the window.

I still had no idea who she was. *Some call me Oya*, she had whispered in my ear, and I didn't know if it was her real name or something she had made up on the spot, and hadn't really cared.

"Nigeria," she said, and I started. I'd been staring out of the window once more, or rather at the beads of water tracing their patterns down the glass. "Then Marrakech, I think. I can't stay in one place for long. It isn't fair."

"You have to ration your company?" My tone suggested I was joking, but the truth of her words chimed somewhere deep inside. She was too good for me. Of course she'd be moving on, to somewhere and probably someone new.

"There are floods," she said. "Sometimes people lose their homes. Sometimes, their lives." She focused on me as she said this last, but I couldn't read her expression.

"The storm." She nodded towards the window, indicating the busy sky, the downpour. "Wherever I am, it must also be."

Her accent was stronger, as if speaking of such things took her – where? Home? I shook my head as her words sank in. What the hell was she saying? She'd told me last night she'd brought the rain for me, but that was a joke, wasn't it? She couldn't have meant it. She couldn't really believe that she'd caused the storm, that it followed her around. The thought struck me again that I didn't really know this woman.

"Where are you from, Oya?"

She didn't answer, just shook her head, a vague expression in her eyes, as if she couldn't quite remember. That was when I truly understood, I think, that she was leaving – and although it seemed inconceivable to be without her after what we had shared, it felt inevitable too. I just wasn't that lucky, and so I told myself it was for the best. She probably did have delusions, problems greater than any I could deal with.

She put her arms around me before she left. Her breath sighed against my throat. There was the faint scent of the world washed clean by rain and the trace of phosphor in her hair, and she was gone.

That night, I couldn't stop thinking about her. The rain had subsided around midday, leaving behind an echoing silence that rang in my ears. Nigeria, she had said. I went online, not really knowing how to look for her, and found myself looking at a tourism website. A ticker in a corner caught my eye with the words: *Flash floods hit Lagos.*

I didn't know what date it had been written so I ran a search for the location and it was right there, a news item about an unbroken spell of fine weather, the threat of water shortages that had been looming – until today. The storm had demolished homes with all the might of a hurricane, but without the warning usually given for such events. Forecasters were trying to recover from accusations of incompetence, talking of a freak in the weather pattern, the impossibility of getting it right all of the time. My gaze went back to the words, *Worst Weather in a Decade.*

I didn't know what to think so I googled her name, as if that would be any use, and was surprised when the results blossomed under my fingers.

Oya was the name of an Orisha, a spirit or deity in the West African Yoruba religion. She was a warrior; she was a woman of passion; she commanded the wind and the lightning and the rain. She was a goddess of fire and of water, a bringer of the storm. She was also a guardian between the worlds of life and death.

I shook my head. Oya probably wasn't even her real name; it was part of her delusion and nothing more. I clicked on a few more links, only half paying attention. Possibly she had heard some last-minute weather report about Nigeria and had followed where it led, or had simply, in her twisted view, struck lucky. Still, with the thought of her still vivid in my mind, the word *coincidence* didn't seem to mean very much.

I half closed my eyes, remembering the scent in her hair, the gleam in her eyes. I wondered if she was out there now, dancing in the warm and unceasing rain.

It was to embark on a sudden flight that I headed out as early as I could the next morning. She had mentioned that Morocco would be next on her list of destinations, or *could* be next, and so I followed. I felt as if I was being drawn in her wake, a man swept off his feet by floodwaters.

I stepped off the plane into the red evening light, heat baking from the ground, and wondered if she had changed her mind and gone elsewhere. Even if she was here, I realised I hadn't the first idea where to find her.

Driving through a dusty haze, I could sense the desert not too far distant, and yet I could also glimpse mountains on the horizon, snow adorning the peaks of the Atlas range. With such variation in climate, would it really be surprising if there should be a storm? But as the taxi reached the outskirts of the city and the sky began to lose its colour, dulling the landscape and the ancient clay walls of Marrakech, it did not feel quite natural: rather, it felt intended.

At the first rumble of thunder, I knew I was in the right place. I dumped my bag at one of the cheaper riads and wandered through the city, passing spice stalls at the edge of the souk, then entering its maze of lanterns, leather goods and brilliantly coloured rugs and carpets. I emerged into the wide open square of Djemaa el Fna just as the rain began to fall – then it hammered the tarps of the food stalls set out for the evening. The tang of barbecue smoke was quelled by the scent of rain. Men rushed to pull plastic sheeting over their pistachios and dried dates. Discordant music was drowned as musicians fled for cover, along with the square's fortune-tellers and henna painters and snake charmers.

Suddenly, in their midst, there she was. Oya wasn't dancing. She stood in the middle of the square, her head flung back, her arms outspread to greet the rain. As I approached and she lowered her eyes to mine, she did not smile; for a fleeting moment, her expression was one of horror.

"You shouldn't have followed," she said. "I shouldn't have told you. It doesn't end well."

For whom, was my first thought – had she done this before, entranced someone then fled? How many times? But she couldn't possibly know how it would end for us. Did it have to end, ever?

I smiled reassuringly, stepping towards her, and after a moment she wrapped her arms around me, nothing between us but her thin red dress. She felt cold, though it didn't seem to trouble her. The square was empty now; the only thing moving was the rain, pounding the cafes and other blocky buildings at its edges.

"Why did you come here?" I asked, though what I meant was: *Why did you leave?*

"I was called here. I am always called."

For some reason, that made me think of something I'd come across when I'd googled her name. "Magicians used to think they could control the wind," I said. "They captured it in bags, thought they could command it with the kind of knots they used, the tightness of the ropes."

I expected her to laugh, but she only looked mournful. She said something in a low voice. I thought it was, *my sisters*.

I waited for her to explain but she shook herself, caught hold of my hand and led me away. The paving teemed and swirled with water, and she laughed, an infectious joy rising from her as she splashed through it like a child jumping in puddles. I wondered again if she was mad, if I had caught a little of her sickness, then pushed the thought aside. It was too big to grapple with and anyway, I didn't want to. I only wanted this: my hand in hers, our fingers slick with rain, the thought of what would follow.

That night, with Oya sleeping next to me, I dreamed. I was with her again in the midst of a storm, the biggest I had yet seen. It filled my consciousness but somehow I knew we weren't on the ground – we were in the heart of it, flying through the black and turbulent air, a world between worlds. Everything smelled of burning; lightning and fire were all about me and I reached for her hand but failed to catch it, or she simply wasn't there any longer – and I started to fall.

I awoke to find her looking at me, already dressed, her eyes full of sadness. "I must go," she said.

Bitterness flooded my mouth; I couldn't stop it from

creeping into my words. "Why? Were you *called?*" I had been there all night. I knew no one had called her, didn't think she even had a phone.

She sighed and looked away. She stood and, without another word, went to the door.

"Wait – Oya, I'm sorry. Wait for me."

"I told you," she said. "It doesn't end well." She walked out of the door and was gone.

It was a marked and sorry lack of fight, I suppose, that made me sit there staring into space instead of running after her, that saw me slinking back to the airport that evening, bag in hand, beaten. I would go home. I would live my life; I would never see her again. I would never dance with her, pressing my lips to hers in the rain, would never again feel that elemental joy. I told myself I didn't care and listened numbly to the announcement – that a number of smaller planes had been grounded because of the storm, which continued to beat at the terminal building, rain bouncing off the runways.

I slumped into my plastic seat. I didn't even know where she'd gone. This time she hadn't told me. I thought about checking weather forecasts, looking for storms, and dismissed the idea. That was madness, wasn't it? Had I really come to believe in her delusion? Besides, how many storms were happening in the world at this very moment? And the ones she'd claimed to raise hadn't even been forecast, had sprung upon the world in a sudden shock, as Oya had upon me.

I looked up, hearing another announcement,

catching the word *Gatwick*, and saw her standing on the opposite side of the waiting area.

I didn't hesitate. For the second time in my life I weaved through a seething crowd towards her, knowing that this time I would never let her go. I stood in front of her, staring into her face. Her eyes were so soft, and with such depths in them – were they mournful? Relieved? Glad? Or everything at once – and she enfolded me in her arms, resting her head on my shoulder, pressing that form that so loved to dance against mine. Her tangled hair smelled of smoke and damp leaves.

"We'll go back," I said, meaning to the city, to the riad. "We'll stay a while. We'll be together."

She pushed herself away without speaking. Still, the slight shake of her head told me everything.

"Then I'll come with you. I'll change my ticket, go wherever you're going."

I peered into her eyes once more and she didn't look away, but I saw the tears brimming there, shining silver-grey in the storm-light, as if the rain was in here too – caressing her, clinging to her. Wanting to hold onto her.

A little later I had a new ticket in my pocket, one that matched hers. I felt certain I was doing the right thing, even more so when the woman at the ticket desk assured us that this flight would not be delayed, that flying in this weather was within the plane's capabilities, and anyway, we would be heading out of the storm.

Oya shifted and fidgeted at my side. I had hurried, almost snatching the ticket before my companion could change her mind and protest. I couldn't lose her again, couldn't bear the idea; that was a void into which I would fall. Surely nothing could be worse than that.

Someone behind us began to talk of a building collapse in Marrakech, of serious flooding, and Oya caught at my arm. Her eyes were wide and anxious, as I had never seen them. Was she, like the city, disintegrating? I told her it was fine, that we'd soon be in the air. She smiled but her expression faded at some new concern, and she flung her arms around my neck.

"I am sorry," she said. "But I must leave. I always do."

I remembered what she'd told me before about how it wasn't fair, her fears that she brought flooding and destruction wherever she went. I soothed her, stroked her hair, told her that everything would be all right. I closed my eyes, sensing the weight it placed upon her, this strange belief that she was some goddess of the storm. And the thought came to me – goddesses demanded sacrifice, didn't they? Yet she only seemed unhappy.

A flash of my dream returned to me: flying through a storm of fire, bigger than anything I had ever known. I opened my eyes, shaking off the vision, and found her face was up close to mine.

"It is glorious," she whispered. "Glorious. But are you sure?"

I was puzzled by her words but, wanting to reassure her, I smiled. As if to show her something truly glorious, I led her to the plate glass windows offering a smeared view of the runway. Out there, the day was failing, the sun nothing but a faint red smear. The sky roiled and shook, its presence felt in a constant rumbling, the bass to the rain's steady percussion. For an instant, a flash of light revealed gigantic banks of cloud, massy and black.

It was like my dream, fire and glory, and I felt a stab of disquiet. It struck me that if she had really spoken the truth, if she was a goddess of the rain, we weren't heading out of the storm at all; we would be taking it with us. We would fly right into its dark and furious heart.

I shook away the thought. It couldn't be real and anyway, that didn't matter; none of it did. I glanced at her. She was here with me now, looking out of this same window, sharing the same moment. We would fly. We would dance.

I stared out as the storm gathered fresh strength and flung it at the earth. Palms whipped in the wind at the farthest edge of the runway, just visible in the ghost-light. I saw it all: the power of it. It was glorious, as she had promised, it was her home, and she would share it with me. I smiled with the joy of it and I tightened my grip on her hand. Everything was as it was supposed to be at last; it was perfect; it was a dark and stormy night.

Slipper

Catriona Ward

It's a dark and stormy night, and I drink three in quick succession. This combination of dark rum and sugar has always been particularly effective. I do not want to retain detail, this evening – want to be nicely blunted for the conflict that's sure to come.

"We leave at nine sharp tomorrow morning," Rachel says. "How much did you have before I got here?" Her fingers play nervously on the stem of her wine glass.

"Not enough. I hate the countryside."

Rachel's finger strokes the back of her ear, the old sign of her irritation. We know how to irk one another, how to hurt. Brothers and sisters do. "You could lay off just this once, Henry," she says. "Couldn't you?"

"I could," I agree. I order another. The waitress comes quickly, as if she had been waiting eagerly for just this moment. It is that stagnant time in August when town is as hot as an empty hell. Surprisingly, the drinks are served correctly, in a highball glass.

"It's a disease," I explain to Rachel. She shakes her head. "You used to be fun. Once upon a time."

"You used to be kind," she replies.

She has come to London for me, I know. She will do

her best to ensure that I arrive at the funeral and remain upright throughout.

As we go into the night, the sky tears open. Rain descends in rippling sheets, great drops of it fall plosive on the cobbles. Thunder cracks the air and then comes lightning. Rachel catches my hand and for a white-lit moment we are small again, frightened animals under a spring storm. Strands of dark hair cling to her wet face as if painted there.

"I don't want to go, R," I say.

"I'm glad," she says. I can scarcely hear her over the hammer of the rain. "Be good for you to do something you don't like, for once."

I lean in close and speak into her ear. "You look much older than you did a year ago," I say. "That sour expression is settling in. You should keep an eye on it."

There is of course no question of me driving. I fall asleep in the passenger seat as we are leaving London, and I wake just as we are turning into the gates of Monkshood. It gives me a nasty jolt of immediacy, as if the house is following me around.

Monkshood is square, white, built on the remains of a medieval priory. It has a cheerful air that belies its name and late inhabitant. The house is surrounded by little woodlands, filled with banks of nodding aconite, the flower they call monkshood. I don't know whether the house was named for the flowers or the monks, or for both.

I wonder, as I approach the front door, if something

will happen when I enter the house; whether it will expel me, send me flying across the lawn. Perhaps I will be consumed by flame. But nothing does happen, and I go in. I sort of wasn't prepared for that.

"You have been busy," I say to Rachel. The house is almost stripped bare. Packing crates and cardboard boxes stand against the walls, filled with books and lumpy bundles of newspaper which I suppose are fragile items – china, ornaments, the mantle clock. I'm to have the contents of the house, and Rachel will have Monkshood itself. She agreed it all with Father, and I couldn't give a damn. She has an affinity for this place, for its ways and moods that borders on the eerie. I wondered whether she might stay, but it seems not.

You could interpret her packing everything up as a generous gesture – to save me trouble. If you didn't know us better, you might indeed think that.

"Here's hoping some fool buyer comes along, and quickly," I say. "Then you and I don't have to see one another again."

I go down into the bowels of the house. I've got to face it sooner or later; it may as well be now.

The basement is cold and white under the glare of the bulb. The shelves that line the walls are empty, exposing the dusty plaster behind. In the south east corner, there is the bricked-up arch that once led to the old cellars, which are all that is left of the priory. I watch the arched doorway, as if something might come through from the dark place beyond, through the brick, through time. I can almost feel Father here. That won't do. I take the water bottle from inside my jacket and drink, eyes watering. That helps.

As children, Rachel and I loved the cellars. They were a maze of old passages and little rooms. There were mice and snails and beetles down there. Sound didn't behave the way it should. We convinced ourselves that the air still smelled like the wine that had been stored there once. But it was probably just damp. We lit candles, made hoods out of sacks and formed a procession of two, walking through the narrow passages, intoning in the guttering light. We did not know any Latin, so we chanted nonsense words.

It was fun to be down there together, the unease walking pleasurably up the back of my neck with its light insect legs. The monks built the cellars, but they had been used by others in the long years since. We found treasure in dark corners. An old silk shoe with a kidskin sole, almost entirely rotted away. A fine length of chain, a ration book.

I never went into the tunnels alone. That would have tipped the balance between pleasure and fear. Rachel wasn't the same. She would spend hours down there, exploring the long stone passages. When I was sent to call her for supper I stood uncertain under the arch, watching the semicircle of light thrown on the uneven flagged passage, and beyond, the dark.

"R," I called, as quietly as possible. I was always afraid, at those times, that something else would answer. The walls threw back my voice in a weird echo. *R, R, R.* Sometimes it was minutes before she replied.

"H." The sound of her footsteps multiplied, became

that of a slow army shuffling towards me in the black. When she appeared, dusty-headed, pupils big with the dark, I was so happy to see her.

"Sorry," she said, stroking my head. "I went too far, that time."

"Don't get lost," I said, clinging to her. "Why do you like it here so much?"

"It teaches me things," she said, thoughtful.

Rachel was fifteen then, I remember that, and it was shortly afterwards that she began sleepwalking.

I was in that elastic place between sleep and waking. I heard footsteps on the landing, passing my door. The tread was far too light to be a person. *Oh, it's just the cat*, I thought. Then I sat upright, because we didn't have a cat.

I seized a torch from the bedside and opened the door. I saw Rachel going down the stairs. I hissed her name and when she didn't answer I followed, feet curling on the cold stone of the entrance hall. She vanished through the little iron-bound door in the corner. I hurried after.

The torch beam danced weirdly over the cluttered basement, showing objects in momentary alarming clarity. I found the opening to the cellars in time to catch Rachel's pink pyjamas disappearing into the dark. I went to the dark mouth and called her name but I knew it would be no good. There was only the empty echo of my voice. It was as if she had been eaten.

I knew, miserable, that I had no choice. I couldn't go in after her. I just couldn't be alone in that place. So I went to wake Father.

We searched all night but it was not until morning

that I found her, curled up behind an old barrel, eyes blank. She was as cold as the dead and something had gnawed at her fingernails, biting them right down to the quick. Her socks had also been eaten through, and her toenails nibbled on. I realised with a little icy shock that it must have been mice.

That was the first time. After the second, Father had the archway filled in and the cellars were closed off for good.

Rachel watched the old gardener do it brick by brick. Later, after they had gone, she stayed, dark eyes still fixed on the glistening, freshly plastered wall. "I don't think that was good idea," she said, shaking her head. "He shouldn't have done it."

"Come up to bed, R," I said.

Her words rang a chime of unease in me. There was something blank and frightening about the solid white place, the door that was not a door, the silent dark behind. The cellars had been eerie when they lay open and crumbling. After Father had them closed off, they became terrifying. Even upstairs, in the hallway on a sunny day, I could still feel the vaulted spaces there beneath our feet, the lonely passages echoing.

Father saw my fear of course. He had an innate cunning, a way of putting his finger on your vulnerable places. I am sure that is why he began to bring me down here to do it.

It still looms in my dreams, his face, the expression it wore at those times. *That will earn you a slippering.* He took it from his foot, burgundy to match his dressing gown. *Bend over, old boy.* The slippering part was over quickly. It was just a rehearsal for the other thing. *Come here, old bean.* It was always *old boy* or *old bean*. He never called me Henry, then. We each became someone else at those times.

Afterwards I would go to the woods. Rachel always found me there.

"He doesn't mean to hurt," she would say. "He never had kindness from his own Papa, you see, so it's not natural to him." She held me tightly. Her arms were warm about my shoulders. Rain dripped from the green leaves and the scent of the earth was all around. It can't have been true, but in these memories the aconites are always in bloom, their delicate purple heads pearled with rain. I wished I could tell her what the slippering really was, but I didn't have the words for such things back then. Perhaps I still don't.

Enough. I shake myself free of memory. Even the here and now is better than that. There's something wet on my face, and my breath keeps catching with a *click* in my throat.

This is exactly what I wanted to avoid. I go upstairs quickly. The packing cases loom in the quiet dusk. To make myself feel better I take something out of a nearby box, wrapped in newspaper. The china makes a grinding sound as it breaks under my foot. It is to be mine, after all. I can do what I like with it. I put the package with its shattered contents carefully back in the crate. Then I go to father's study.

"You're out of luck," Rachel says. She sits in the window seat, swinging her leg. Her hair falls long and dark down her back. There is grey in it, I see now. I was just trying to rattle her, last night, but I wasn't entirely wrong. She looks worn away, like her face is being eroded. "The decanter, the glasses, the whiskey, the brandy," she says. "They were the first things I packed up. Sorry, H. Kill yourself if you like. I won't be a part of it."

I mime despair. It is infuriating that she has anticipated me – but after all, we have always known to expect the worst of one another.

I have an emergency bottle in my bag but I'm not going to tell her that.

I sleep on a mattress on the sitting room floor. All the bedrooms are full of boxes, the beds broken down into pieces, leaning against the wall. I can't help but suspect that this is Rachel's way of delivering her message – that I have no place at Monkshood. Really, she needn't have bothered. I was born in this house but I never felt at home here.

Images drift through my mind. A red spaniel's tail, Father's silver headed walking stick. He lost his leg in the Great one, which didn't stop him going back for the second. I think they let him sit behind a desk for number two. He must have hated that, almost as much as he hated being a parent. Perhaps we could all have been perfectly happy if Mother had lived. He could have shot and walked the dogs and drunk brandy and soda and never seen us at all. But she died and by some terrible mishap the money died with her, or at least it went back to America, which was just as bad. So he couldn't pay for help or the kind of school that would take us out of his sight.

I don't remember her. I think Rachel does, just.

They wake me in the night, the long shining needles of pain. I set my teeth and manage not to make a sound. Real pain is a private thing; I won't have Rachel's eyes on me. It sweeps through again, stabbing at my eyes, my head, my heart and along the length of my limbs. My jaw clenches so hard that I feel a shard of molar come away on my tongue.

The vodka trickles into my mouth through my teeth. It's the worst thing I could do for the pain, of course, but it is the only thing that helps. At length the agony recedes, or maybe I get used to it. It is a recent development, the alcoholic neuropathy, a sign that matters are reaching a crisis.

I wake to the sound of the world breaking. It's so loud that it seems to almost be inside me. I raise a bleary head. The noise comes again from below.

At first, I think that the basement is filled with fog. Actually, the air is white with dust. It tickles my nostrils with its dead chalky scent. Through the swirling clouds I can see a figure clothed in white overalls, wearing goggles like the eyes of a great insect. I call out and the figure pauses mid swing, jackhammer raised above its head.

"What are you doing?" I ask again, although that is fairly clear. The hole in the cellar wall is like a jagged mouth, rounded in surprise or a scream. What I meant to ask was, *why?*

The white figure lowers the jackhammer to the ground. It raises the goggles to show Rachel's brown eyes, ringed with plaster dust. "Go and help yourself to coffee," she says. "It's in the kitchen."

"It's something to do with probate," she says, spreading butter on toast with a shaking hand. There are blisters on her palm where she gripped the hammer. The morning light is cruel on her parchment skin. "Naturally, Father didn't have permission to brick up that arch. The surveyors will have to get in and look at the foundations to value it. This house is built on a bloody honeycomb."

She eats the toast in three quick bites, teeth clicking, and then rises. Her old black dress is too big for her now, the neckline shows her sharp, carved-out collarbones. "Are you ready?"

The important thing at funerals is not to allow oneself to feel too much. You've got to be careful, or you will leave a piece of yourself in the grave with the dead. My feelings aren't about father, of course, but that won't save me.

We aren't the only ones in church, but almost. The solicitor who drew up the will is here from the village. He has a comically old-fashioned little moustache, like a neat pair of apostrophes painted on his top lip. He is nervous and his eyes are young. There are two neighbours, women, who I don't know. They must have moved here since I left. They have come for curiosity, I suspect, rather than affection. We don't go to the graveside after the service, Rachel decided that. And suddenly, it's over.

The young solicitor comes back to Monkshood, as do the curious neighbours. The day is beautiful, flooded with sunlight. Along the drive, the aconites are coming into bloom.

Rachel has made a clearing in the forest of boxes and

crates, large enough for us all to stand with a tea and a biscuit. It is cramped and there is nowhere to put our cups down so we talk and drink, hunched over them.

"I'm Tom Orland," the solicitor says. "Of Orland and Orland." I can't take my eyes from his little moustache. "Your father's executor. Will it be convenient after tea?"

I shrug. "I refer you to my sister," I say. "She's in charge. None of this has anything to do with me."

One of the women tells me how beautiful the house looks today. "My father was keen on local history," she says. "Monkshood was fascinating to him. Nothing was ever built here, due to some old protection about common land – I can't remember exactly what. Such a waste, it's a lovely position. Then your grandfather got around the bylaw somehow and built the house."

"Well, there was the priory here before all that," I say. "Monkshood stands on its foundations."

"No," she says, puzzled. "There was certainly never a priory in these parts."

"How strange," I say politely and excuse myself to the lav. It is unwise to leave it too long between nips.

The women leave reluctantly after an hour or so, craning brightly round corners, eyes guessing the shapes of shrouded furniture, wrapped objects. "What a lovely scent," one of them says. "Is it pot pourri?" She's right, I can smell it too: something heavy and rich, like wine.

We perch awkwardly on the boxes in the study and Tom Orland takes out the will. He reads slowly and stumbles a little. I have already had rather a lot from my emergency bottle today, and I'm sitting in a patch of warm sunlight. I find my mind drifting, moving outside, lightly borne on the summer day, over the tops of the apple trees in the orchards. Below me the young green grass, the rushing stream, glimpses of blossom.

I am brought back by Rachel's scream. She is pale and trembling, one hand over her mouth, staring at Orland. "That cannot be right," she says.

"Those are the terms," he replies. "The contents of the house are yours, but Monkshood is left to Henry."

"Damn you, Henry." Her voice is a high rasp. "This very last thing, you couldn't help taking it too."

"I am as surprised as you." To the solicitor I say, "It doesn't have to change anything. We can sell it, just as Rachel was planning to. I'll give her the money."

"You aren't permitted to sell, or leave it vacant," Orland says. "I'm terribly sorry, but unless you agree to live at Monkshood it will go to a trust for wounded soldiers."

My brain is fogged with surprise and vodka. "I don't understand," I say. "Why would Father want me to live here?"

Rachel stares at me. Then a smile spreads across her face. It is too wide, like a cut made by a knife. She begins to laugh.

"Stop," I say. "Please. God, Rachel."

"I see it now," she says. "He's not giving the house to you. He's giving you to Monkshood. What's left of you, that is." She makes for the door, gasping with tears. When I try to stop her, she shoves me and I lose my balance and fall hard among the boxed remains of Father's life.

I find Rachel at our place in the woods. She is hugging her knees and staring into nothing. The birds sing in the trees around us, a riot of life.

I sit down beside her. "Let the soldiers have it," I say. "We'll manage somehow. You could come back to town with me."

"No," she says,

"Oh, come," I say. "How much would it really have fetched, this old pile?"

"I wasn't going to sell it," Rachel says. "I was going to burn it. Do you never wonder why the aconites are always in bloom, here?

"They're not," I say. But I stop for a moment, struck by doubt. Perhaps she is right.

"Oh, H," she says, furious. "You are wilfully blind. You never want to face up to things."

"Steady," I say. But I have a numb feeling like the creep of frostbite.

"It lives in the cellars," she says. "Though they're not cellars, not really. It is old and it doesn't understand that everyone it knew is dead. If you decide to live in the house, you're going to have to give it things. People. Father offered up mother, and after that he gave you – at least, the part of you that mattered."

"No one gave me to anyone," I say. "I'm right here."

"Are you?" Rachel's touch is cool on my cheek. "Don't be so sure, H. It eats all kinds of things."

I feel very drunk, and I wonder if perhaps this is all a hallucination. But I have a horrible feeling that it's not. It seems like something I have always known. "What is it?" I ask. "Does it have a name?"

"I don't know," she says. "Maybe. I had my own name for it. It always spoke to me when Father took you to the basement. I could hear the beating and the sound mingled with its voice. So, when I was very little, I called it Slipper." She takes my face in her cool hands and looks. Her eyes are long and dark. "The thing is H, what's left for me, even if I get free of it? What is there for you? Where do we belong?"

And here we are at last in the final place; the secret that lies at the heart of us both.

It was after one of those times, when Rachel was comforting me in the woods, that it first happened between us. I was sixteen, she seventeen. I could sense that I was growing too old for Father. He called me to the basement less frequently, but it had the violence of disappointment. It had been a bad one, that day. I remember rising above my body. I felt my limbs flying apart, each to a different corner of the room. When I got to the woods I was still weeping, and all the feelings were running into one another.

Rachel found me there. She held me and cried a little too. She asked me again and again what was wrong. I couldn't tell her. So I did the next best thing and tried to speak to her through touch. The curve of her cheek, the long sweep of her lashes, the mole on her wrist – her body is mapped forever in my mind. A long-ago journey, which we never speak of. When I came to the glade that day, I felt that nothing about my person belonged to me anymore. But the moment I touched Rachel, I owned myself again.

I started it, I know. But it is something we did together. It is still the best thing that ever happened to me, and I suspect to her too, which is why we cannot forgive one another.

"You're right," I say, and take her hand. "We only belong together." Is this happening now, or then? The past and the present overlie one another. The blinding blue of the aconites is painful to my eyes, my heart. We are enclosed in a circle of us. It has the feeling of something written long ago, and out of our control.

We stand before the crumbling archway. Piles of broken brick litter the floor. The scent of wine is rich in the air. I don't know what time it is, or even what day. We were a long time in the glade. Stars wheeled overhead, and dawn came twice, I think. But now it is time to act.

"We have a gift for you," Rachel says to the dark. "It's the greatest gift you can be given, because it is surrendered willingly. And in return you have to promise to go to sleep for a long, long time." She looks thin and frightened, and very young. I take her hand.

"Do you promise?" Rachel asks. The dark seems to pulse. It reaches out like a hand towards us its breathing deep and long. How did I not hear it all those years?

"Was that a yes?" I whisper to Rachel.

She shakes her head. "It doesn't matter," she says. "It lies."

I flick on my torch. We walk hand in hand into the dark. As we go through the tunnels, the old walls breathe about us. I tighten my grip on her hand.

"Not just yet," she whispers. The scent of wine is strong, now, it encloses us like smoke. I can smell what is underneath – the liquid stench of rot.

We reach an open space in the deepest part of the tunnel. A cave. This is further, deeper than I have ever been. Or perhaps it wasn't here when we both came exploring as children. Maybe this part of the maze is just for Rachel.

The chamber is lit by some unseen source. I turn off the torch. The paintings on the uneven rock walls seem to dance, the men with spears chase the great deer through the flickering light. Many crude wooden racks are scattered across the cave floor, hung with drying skins. Pelts are stretched across tables. Some are the hides of animals. Some are not. I can see the flattened outline of a nose, the creased skin of a knuckle, the light down of a young man's chest.

In the centre of the chamber there is a hole. It is from this hole that the breathing comes. As we approach, the sweet rotten scent intensifies until I am choking with it. I can hear its voice, now – it is filled with the sound of beaten flesh and my father's grunting. *Slipper.*

I take the matches from my pocket, and my emergency bottle from beneath my coat. There is a petrol-soaked rag in the neck of the bottle. I light it and throw the flaming bottle into the dark hole. There is a roar and then comes a noise so great that it sounds like silence. Rachel and I look at one another. The world grows wide and white and we are truly together at last.

All the Secret Colours of the World

Simon Avery

It was a dark and stormy night when I met Alison. We were both sheltering outside the entrance to Hillingdon A&E, lost in the London suburbs. A friend of mine had fallen down a flight of stairs after too much booze, leaving him bruised and concussed; they were keeping him in overnight for observation. I'd promised I'd return tomorrow to collect him. I was outside, about to light my last cigarette, staring out at the rain and the remains of Saturday night, feeling a bit lost, a bit aimless. I'd come to London for a change of scene, hoping that life here would sweep me up in its wake and lead me to whatever the next phase of my life would be. So far the city had left me wanting. Right until that moment. And then, there it was: Life with a capital L. The gravity of it, returning me to the world I knew. *Come back*, it said. *We're not done with you yet.*

I heard Alison's voice first; she was on the phone, seeking help. She was dressed for a night on the town: an obligatory little black dress and heels. She ended her call and glanced at me speculatively, rubbing the back of her neck. "Do you have a cigarette?" she asked.

I showed her the packet. "Last one." I hadn't lit it yet. I offered it to her.

She smiled, her head bowed, face hidden behind long blonde curls, and shook her head. "I couldn't."

"Yeah, you could."

After a moment she took the cigarette and lit it, still rubbing her neck, rolling her shoulders with a grimace.

"I didn't realise that there was such a strict dress code here on a Saturday night," I said. "If I'd known I'd have worn my cummerbund and spats."

Alison had been on her way into the city when some dick in a BMW had ploughed into the back of her Range Rover. She thought she had whiplash, so she'd driven herself to A&E. "I've tried calling friends, but they're all otherwise occupied," she said. "Saturday night and the storm and everything."

"I can wait with you, if you want," I offered.

She sized me up for a moment, trying to make a snap decision on a stranger. "Don't you have anywhere else to go?"

I laughed. "Tragically, no."

After half an hour they called Alison in to see a doctor. He examined her and was concerned about the pain she was still feeling in her neck when he moved across various pressure points. She came out looking very pale. "They want to x-ray me," she said. "Will you stay with me until it's done?"

"Of course," I said.

They placed Alison in a neck brace and strapped her head down on a gurney, which alarmed us both. She reached for my hand while we sat waiting in a back room and I smiled and squeezed it tightly. The hospital was quiet; just the soft hiss of nurses' shoes moving across the floor beyond the curtain. Muttered conversation. A feeling of hovering outside of the world for a moment, waiting breathlessly to re-enter.

Luckily the x-rays showed that there was no damage done to Alison's neck. They gave her some pain relief and, once we were outside, I offered to drive her home. There was another moment of quick and quiet deliberation, and then she led me to her Range Rover on the other side of the car park. I left my Volvo behind. I had to pay a hefty fine when I retrieved it the next day.

Alison lived near Heathrow Airport. Her place was on the other side of the M25, in the indistinct area where the city and the countryside fray into one another. The roar of traffic on the London Orbital, and of planes taking off and landing, were its invariable background noise. I wondered how she slept with that much noise going on. I'd grown up on the coast of Dorset; I was a country boy at heart. You'd open the windows and all you heard was the sweet-as-nectar sound of ocean and seagulls. But once Alison closed the door on her architect-designed dream home, all that remained was silence. It was divided over four levels, with balconies on the first, second and top floor, revealing dramatic views of London after dark. I walked around while she went to change, picking things up, staring at them then putting them back down. A pair of kicked-off Vivienne Westwood shoes in the hall. A full and varied wine rack. African fabric draped over the couches. Persian rugs on the polished reclaimed elm flooring. Several classic Eames chairs. I believe they call it tasteful eclecticism. I felt like I was making the place look untidy. Low-level class anxiety. Although I owned my house in Dorset, I'd always worked menial jobs; my education (or lack thereof) precluded me from climbing too high. Consequently my contact with people like Alison was minimal.

Her photography, which adorned many of the walls, seemed to apprehend some hitherto undiscovered aspect in each of her subjects. These were faces I'd seen on magazine covers and on the screen for years. There was something raw in these black and white portraits. Something of the true life of these men and women, being gently exposed for all to see. It was like a magic trick.

We made supper and sat out on one of the balconies watching the electrical storm raging across London's skyline. The lights of planes emerged from the clouds and descended, out of sight on the other side of the motorway. Later I noticed there were other photos around the house, these much more candid, clearly of Alison's daughter, Samantha. Walking down a hallway, I could watch her grow up in black and white, from a toddler to a teenager. The same elusive eyes of her mother, the same wild blonde curls. The pictures were filled to the brim with love. But there was something else. I couldn't place it at first, but then the truth of it sidled up to me, accosted me.

There was so much *space* in here. So much sad, empty space. The place was freighted with the residual ache of human geography. I knew what was coming before Alison told me.

"Samantha died a few months ago," she said. "They

found her in a verge at the side of the road, near junction 15 of the M25. About a mile away from here."

"Oh, God," I said. I sat forward without thinking. She was close enough for me to console, but it was too soon for that. Instead I just said, "I'm so sorry," and shook my head at the inadequacy of language in those moments.

"This is too much, isn't it?" Alison said. "We don't know each other."

"It's OK," I said. "Tell me."

"There was an inquest. Sudden cardiac death, they called it. But she had no underlying heart problems. *Nothing* like that at all. The police questioned a man called Alan Fletcher. A witness had seen Samantha talking to him in a cafe a week before she was found dead."

"Alan Fletcher," I said. "Not the property developer who was on that TV show?"

"Yes, that's him." Alison rose and fetched a folder that contained print-outs and newspaper clippings, SAMANTHA scribbled across its cover. I felt for her; the near impossible task for a mother to let go of her daughter. She took out a report from the Evening Standard.

Businessman detained by police investigating the death of Samantha Ackroyd.

Property developer and TV celebrity Alan Fletcher was detained two days ago by police investigating the death of 16-year-old Samantha Ackroyd.

> *Two years ago, Artemis Construction Group, Fletcher's property development firm, entered administration. An uncertain market, a string of loss-making contracts and accounting irregularities were seemingly to blame. Not long after administrators were called in Fletcher was detained under Section 2 of the Mental Health Act after family members became alarmed at his erratic behaviour. Fletcher's wife, Marion, divorced him in 2017, relocating to Switzerland with their two children soon after. Fletcher's brother, Steven, has overseen the sales of his brother's properties and assets, including his estate in Buckinghamshire, which includes the Grade 1 listed Hawtrey House.*
>
> *Upon release, Fletcher went missing for over a year, but was witnessed talking to Samantha Ackroyd in a cafe in the village of Harmondsworth a week prior to her death. Fletcher was interviewed, but he was later released.*

"Do you know what happened to him?"

Alison suddenly looked cross with herself to be talking about him at all. "Fletcher? He lives in a caravan now, from what I've heard."

"Do you think he was responsible?"

She looked at me, her eyes glassy. "Maybe indirectly?" She shook her head. "I honestly don't know."

"It's OK," I said.

"I've thrown myself into my work these past couple of

months, just to avoid being here. But you can't run away from that kind of thing, can you? It follows you around, wherever you go." Alison sniffed, rubbed at her eyes angrily. "Christ, *sorry!* This isn't casual conversation anymore, is it?"

"It's perfectly fine," I said. I knew all about grief – I'd lost my wife to leukaemia. She was three months pregnant with our first child when we found out. The doctor had recommended we abort the child in order for Emily to begin chemotherapy. But there were complications, and I had to live with losing a child and a wife in the same year. I'd spent years running away from it and standing still at the same time. Moving from one place to another. Restless in my own skin.

Later on, I told her all of this, because it was easy with Alison. Usually you save the heavy shit for a later date, but we had it all out on the table before midnight. It was weirdly liberating, like starting with the hard questions first and working your way backwards. We talked about the things we did to switch off. She liked Tom Waits and the smell of freshly cut lavender. Her favourite authors were Richard Yates and Margaret Atwood. She liked Ingmar Bergman movies, and old re-runs of Columbo. She loved to visit old European cities and take pictures of architecture.

Her old man had been a professional photographer too, a contemporary of Brian Duffy and David Bailey. She had some of his work from the swinging sixties displayed upstairs: all micro-dresses, 'It' girls and effortless cool. Jean Shrimpton, Jane Birkin, Michael Caine… Alison had grown up in that rarefied air, playing in her dad's studio while John Lennon and Yoko Ono tramped through, teasing her and spending their tea breaks on the floor, playing with her. She had some quite excellent stories.

We talked until it was getting light, moving from one room to the next, settling for a while as we discussed our lives, then relocating again. We'd quickly relaxed around each other, and I discovered that Alison had an earthy sense of humour. I found myself wanting to amuse her, just to hear her husky, throaty laugh, and to lift her away from the quiet dismay of her life these past few months. I didn't have much to offer, but I had that, at the very least. She asked me to massage her neck for a while, and then finally, we fell asleep on her couch while the air turned cool, then warm again. At ten, I made us breakfast and then called for a cab, bracing myself for the fine on my Volvo, which was still sitting at Hillingdon A&E. At the door we hesitated briefly, then she pulled me close, stood on her tip-toes and kissed me on the mouth. A gentle but firm affirmation that we both wanted the same thing, even though we were labouring under the weight of circumstance. *Life, with a capital L.* But you can't stop. Life doesn't wait. Why should you?

We took it steady for the first couple of months, acutely aware of the eggshells we were treading on. I accompanied her on a couple of photo-assignments, one of them in Paris. The shoot was interminable. A couple of models in next to nothing, posing beside the Seine at the height of summer. I tried making conversation with them, but they were too cool, too remote, too French.

In Alison's downtime, we held hands and did what couples had done in Paris for hundreds of years: we let the city seduce us. The bright lights of the *bateaux mouches* on the Seine as they cruised towards the *Île de la Cité*. Tourists waving from the decks at the people on the bridge. The golden buildings of *Sainte-Chappelle* and *Notre Dame*. Dinner at *Café de Paix*. Standing on a concrete terrace with a perfect view of *La Tour Eiffel*; more tourists, all poised with cameras and mobile phones held aloft. By the time it was dark, the light was shifting across the vaulted sky, dipping in the currents of the Seine far below us. We embraced it all. And we kissed like it was going out of fashion.

Here it was easy to put the past in a box and walk away from it like it didn't exist. But then you realised it was you in the box, and you had to get out.

One weekend we drove out to Hawtrey House, Alan Fletcher's old estate – ostensibly so that Alison could take some photos, although I later discovered that she had ulterior motives. She was afraid that I'd think she was obsessed with what had really happened to Samantha. I didn't. I could only guess at how difficult these past few months had been for her.

The gates were solidly locked but Alison was already clambering over the wall before I had a chance to prevaricate. We had to walk almost three miles through dense woodland before we reached the house. It was an imposing Grade 1 listed country pile set in the centre of a 4,500 acre estate in the Buckinghamshire countryside, dating back to the late sixteenth century. It looked like the setting for a lavish BBC costume drama.

By 1998 several multi-million pound property deals both here and abroad had enabled Alan Fletcher to lay down a reported 10 million pounds to buy the estate. Twenty years later, his family and business was gone, leaving his life in disarray. I was astonished at how quickly something could begin to crumble and decay. Houses, business ventures, families... Sometimes no amount of love and care can retrieve something that's built on uncertain foundations.

We spent several hours that morning exploring the grounds and interior of Hawtrey House. 103 rooms, clad in blocks of Bath stone. We wandered through grand drawing rooms, lined with marble, climbed sweeping staircases decorated with wrought iron art nouveau scrollwork. In the vast ballroom, a wall of floor to ceiling windows had been shattered by vandals, the glass crunching beneath our shoes. There was a dreamlike, deeply melancholy nature to the place. After an hour you could feel it seeping into your bones. A repository of history, the bricks aching with captive memory.

Alison didn't want to talk when she had her camera in her hands. I carried her bag of lenses for the Leica she was using today. After an hour or so, we took a break. In the centre of the house was a huge courtyard, turned into a huge winter garden atrium room. The large fronds of dead tropical plants wilted across the glass and underfoot. The wild had claimed it for itself.

"Have you noticed the graffiti?" Alison said after a while.

"Yeah," I said. "It's everywhere. What about it?"

"Specific graffiti, dummy. Some of it is tagged."

"Tagged?"

"Christ, how *old* are you? A tag is the graffiti artists' signature."

"The extent of my graffiti knowledge begins and ends with Banksy."

"There's this artist called Mojo Pin."

"And?"

Alison got to her feet and held out her hand. "Come on, old timer. Follow me."

Being of a 'certain age', most graffiti looks the same to me. But once Alison told me what to look for, I could see the difference with Mojo Pin's work.

"Look," Alison said. "See that?"

They were statements, some of them quite plain, others somewhat more ambiguous. You had to follow the words as they spiralled inwards to a centre burning with colours.

You are a still point in a turning world.

We are at the edge,

where your future is auditioned.

Once I knew what I was looking for, we moved quickly through the rooms, looking for more. It was a strangely addictive process.

In the bastard countryside

we may be transformed.

At the time I didn't understand what Mojo Pin was getting at, but clearly this was more than casual graffiti. These were statements of intent. Lines being drawn in the metaphysical sand.

"What's the 'bastard countryside'?" I asked.

"It's the edge-land," Alison said. "That place between the city and the countryside. It's where they build business parks and allotments and motorways. Part man-made, part natural."

"And you know this how?"

"I think it's tied in with Samantha. This..." She indicated the graffiti. "*This* is connected to Samantha. She contacted Mojo Pin not long before she died. I knew this graffiti was here. I just wanted to see it first-hand. I thought it might help me understand."

At the confluence

we can be changed forever.

"I need you to explain all of this to me," I said while we sat, listening to birds singing in the eaves of the house. The unfinished aspect of Samantha's death was still clinging to Alison, ensuring that the wound was never properly healed. I took Alison's hand. "Explain it all and if I can help in *any* way, I promise you that I will."

Alison looked at me, her eyes wet with tears. She squeezed my hand and smiled. I felt our relationship shift then; that subtle transformation to something deeper and more resonant. If I could have bottled that look and saved it forever, I would have. Finally she nodded, and we packed up and went home.

I contacted Mojo Pin last night. <u>She</u> called me back – colour me amazed to discover that Mojo Pin is <u>actually a woman</u>! Fucking hell. I spent a week trying to decide how to approach her, what to tell her, etc. I had no idea if I could trust her with what I had to say. I haven't told Mum any of this. She wouldn't understand what's going on in my life right now, wouldn't understand why I didn't just go to the police. I know she'd only want to help, but this is about more than just Daniel now. It's about what happened to him and what can happen to me too.

I just know that this isn't me. That I'm in transition somehow. I've been having these <u>seriously</u> fucking psychedelic dreams about becoming something else.

Mojo Pin calls it 'looking for the pearl in the flesh of the oyster'. She says it's a process, not an event.

She gave me the number of a guy she's heard from. Some rich dude who lost his mind (which isn't very reassuring, but still). He's undergoing the same process. And he knows about the place where IT happened. Mojo Pin calls them 'liminal points'. Apparently people have been searching for these places, or have been drawn to them since time began. They either get changed or they move through them to 'break on through to the other side'.

Anyway, this guy. Alan Fletcher. I've arranged to go and meet him tomorrow. He sounded really fucking weird on the phone. I'll report back afterwards.

"I felt like I'd had my head buried in the sand all this time," Alison said, after she'd shown me Samantha's blog. Prior to that post the entries were fairly standard adolescent fare. There was nothing afterwards.

"You couldn't know what was going on in your kid's brain. Teenagers. They have this whole other life in their mind while they're figuring shit out."

"But this was big," Alison said.

"Sure, it *sounded* big," I said. "But they feel like they're moving huge furniture around in their head. That's what they do until life sets in. You have no idea what this 'transition' is that she was talking about," I said. "It wasn't a gender thing, was it?"

"No, it wasn't that." Alison shook her head. "I thought I *understood* my kid. I thought she knew she could talk to me about anything. *Anything...*"

"And this Daniel? You'd never met him? He wasn't a boyfriend or something?"

"I'd no idea. I thought she'd have told me if she was seeing a boy... Maybe I didn't know my daughter at all. The police say he went missing. They never found him. Before they saw this blog, they hadn't drawn any kind of connection between him and Samantha."

We sat together on Samantha's bed and stared at the room. There were posters for bands I didn't recognise. A dressing table, a CD player, some old cuddly toys from childhood on a shelf, a wardrobe stuffed with clothes, a bookcase overflowing with books. I'd looked through them earlier. Beside the standard fare, there were books by Iain Sinclair, Will Self, Robert MacFarlane... After some research I could draw a rough connection between the blog posts and Mojo Pin and aspects of these writers. Psychogeographical roaming. The narrative of letting a journey take you to where the past exists beneath the present, waiting to be dusted off and understood again. But I didn't know where that had ultimately led Samantha, other than to a lonely death at the side of the M25.

"Did the police look into Mojo Pin?"

"I'm not sure. They found the blog posts. I didn't know a thing about them, but I don't think they took them seriously." Alison shrugged. "Anyway, I tried searching online for her, but how do you find a graffiti artist? No one really knows who Banksy is, do they?"

"Let's see," I said. I placed Samantha's laptop on my knees and typed Mojo Pin's name into a search engine. We looked at the results in the photos first. By now her style was immediately distinctive. Those cryptic messages and statements of intent, spiralling into a centre alive with colour.

We finally uncovered a brief interview with Mojo Pin, along with a small photograph taken in a room where one of the walls was covered in Post-it notes and maps, pins with thread connecting points of interest, drawing conclusions. Mojo Pin was wearing a hoodie and ski goggles, which managed to obscure all but the lower portion of her face, so that she could retain her anonymity. The only real point of interest in the interview was this statement:

I like to think that I'm part of a scattered community that circles a common centre. We're all searching for a locus point so we can enact change...

I think if you cast focus on something for long enough, it unseats the layers of time there. The fabric of the place begins to oscillate. It becomes disrupted, emotionally, physically, politically. It's like the dérive. You keep walking until your relationship with a location changes, until you finally see something that until that moment was hidden. But it was always there. You understand? It was waiting until we were ready to raise our consciousnesses and engage.

We didn't get much further that night. Information on the graffiti artist was scarce. Usually there's something there, some thread to pull at until you find whatever it is that you want, but not that night. The solution was staring us in the face, but I didn't see it until later.

By which point our lives had changed forever.

"For a couple of weeks now I've wanted to tell you that, well, I *love* you. But I know that's fraught with all sorts of shit for both of us. We've heard it before, we've *said* it before. Samantha's dad was an absolute *bastard*, but my little girl came out of that relationship, so I wouldn't change something that went bad on me because I got her out of it...

"But still... it's like this big *bold* statement in neon letters, isn't it? Goodbye to all that simple business – you know, holding hands and driving out into the country. Sex on Sunday mornings. Instead it's hello to something more permanent. And neither of us does permanent very well."

"Alison?"

"Yes?"

"I love you too."

"Oh."

"And again with a bit more enthusiasm."

"That's *good*. OK then."

"Good."

"That makes the next thing a bit easier to say. But I don't want you to think I trapped you into anything. *Shit*. I probably should have said all of this the other way around."

"I'm a big boy, Alison. I think I can handle the heavy shit too."

"OK."

"What is it?"

"Well, I checked twice. Two different tests to make sure. Apparently I'm pregnant."

"Oh."

"And again with a bit more enthusiasm."

"Alison?"

"Yes?"

"I love you."

Life has a habit of pushing everything non-essential to the side in order to service the more important aspects of our existence. The twelve-week scan rolled around. We sat holding hands in the reception of a brightly decorated ante-natal clinic in Uxbridge. I could feel my heart beating, very fast, very loud. We kept each other talking, aware that we were both wrestling with our own stumbling blocks surrounding the pregnancy. Apart from the increased risk of being pregnant at the age of 42, for Alison there was this feeling of betraying Samantha's memory somehow. That she was moving on too fast with the rest of her life, abandoning her child while there was still some mystery surrounding her death.

I had a – probably wholly irrational – fear of what we'd find during the ultra-sound. I couldn't shake the memory of sitting in rooms like these with my wife when she'd been diagnosed with leukaemia. Days of quiet dismay, of losing the ability to speak, to say anything of worth that could encompass the vastness of the horror that filled our days. Nothing was changed but everything was. We'd move through our house, the rooms altered beyond comprehension, beyond knowing. Even then, I was clinging desperately to the faint hope that we could claw our way back to something approaching normalcy. But then we had to abort the baby in order for Emily to have any kind of hope of saving herself, and then, a few months later, she was taken from me too. And I knew on the day I returned from the hospital for the final time that the rooms of our home were transformed indelibly. They would have to belong to someone new for them to hold any kind of meaning again. Perhaps that was what Mojo Pin had been getting at. Everywhere is a palimpsest; a time capsule of layers of meaning, much of it unintelligible without context. But the emotions lay dormant there, encased in history. Perhaps you could access those points, perhaps certain places attracted extremes of violence, or sadness, or joy. Perhaps there were endless reservoirs of power there that could change the environment or transform you into something else.

We followed a young sonographer, Kerry, into a small room whose windows faced a small courtyard with a solitary cherry tree in its centre. The morning was warm; we were still clinging to the last tatters of a substantial English summer, which filled the room with a rosy golden glow that seemed to fan at the embers of my anxiety. Alison lay back on the freshly papered bed and rolled up her t-shirt while Kerry closed the blinds and seated herself at the ultrasound's control panel. I sat down, wondering how many people sat in this room, hearing good news and bad news, in a day, a week, a month, a year. A holograph of joy and anguish, repeating itself over the years. Could you mine that raw emotion and make something of it?

I held Alison's hand and my breath until Kerry was satisfied and finally angled the monitor towards us. Part of me was still trapped in an event years in the past, similar to this one, but with tragic results. But then I was looking at the screen, at the black and silver clouds, contracting and parting as the probe moved across Alison's belly. Kerry located the uterus, and then the placenta, zooming in, the picture resolving as the fabric of what was alive within Alison began to oscillate. Waiting for me to raise my consciousness and *engage*.

❖

Birmingham was about an hour and a half up the M40. We rose early, working around the morning sickness. I'd tried to insist I could do this by myself, but Alison wouldn't hear of it. If we were going to talk to Mojo Pin, then she had long-gestating questions of her own; she wanted to know what the artist and Samantha had talked about; she wanted, I think, to be able to look the woman in the eye. She'd feel the truth of things if they were there to be found.

The night before I'd looked at the interview with Mojo Pin again, drawn to the grainy photograph, aware that something about it was stirring an insight in my mind. It was hard not to get side-tracked by the strangeness of the wall of Post-It notes and maps, but I realised that there was something through the window that I recognised. I'd lived in Birmingham during my marriage to Emily – we'd had a good twenty-odd years there in the suburbs. So when I saw the golden dome on top of the minaret on the Highgate mosque, I knew I could work out exactly where that room was. It was just a case of working out the angle of the mosque in relation to the window, drawing a line on my OS map, then going to Google Street View and pinpointing the address. It was in a row of flats above shops, just around the corner from the mosque. So we decided to drive up there on the off-chance that we'd find her willing to speak to us. It was clearly a long-shot but, as the weeks went on, and our baby grew, we both realised the absolute necessity of solving the riddle of Samantha's death.

The small shopping parade in Highgate was an urban area that had managed to avoid any kind of care from the council. It was dirty and broken-down, a tired-out remnant of the seventies. Industrial factories and council housing and flats. Car exhausts roaring and exploding, empty faces staring at us as they drifted past. It didn't seem like the kind of place to bring an expectant mother, but before I could express my concerns, Alison was out of the Volvo and looking for steps up to the flats above the row of shuttered shop fronts. But there was no one at home. We knocked on the door for a couple of minutes, and then accepted defeat. I decided to bring the car around the back, where I could protect the sanctity of my wheels, and we could keep an eye out for the artist returning. We'd accepted it was a gamble coming up here, but there was this sense of Mojo Pin being a missing cog in the machinery that had swept up Alison's child and left her abandoned by the roadside at the end of everything. It felt for the moment like we were grasping at ghosts.

Mojo Pin came home after five in the afternoon. We'd sat in the car for three hours, which isn't wholly advisable for a pregnant woman. Save for a couple of trips to the local McDonald's for toilet breaks and lunch and to stretch our legs, we'd kept watch on the flat. We didn't realise it was her until she took out her keys and stopped in front of her door. She was wearing a hoodie, but her long russet hair was loose, and her pale freckled face on display. She was slight, no older than 25. I don't know what I was expecting. It was slightly jarring, like seeing a superhero unmasked.

Alison was out the door. I caught her up on the steps. Pregnant women take *forever* on steps. I wasn't expecting an answer when we knocked on the door again, but after a moment, there she was. Beneath the hoodie was a well-cut pin-stripe jacket and skirt. I hadn't considered that Mojo Pin probably had a normal 9 to 5 job – data entry administrator by day, graffiti artist with a preponderance for ambiguous axioms by night. You can kick against the pricks, but on your *own* time. She looked even younger than I'd first thought. There was a guarded quality there, understandable considering where she lived and what she did in her spare time.

"We need to talk to you," Alison said in a firm tone. "I'm Alison Ackroyd. I'm Samantha's mum."

I saw the immediate conflict in her eyes. A quickening of breath. Acutely aware of the minefield that she was about to go walking through.

"I know my daughter contacted you before she died," Alison went on. "I know you're Mojo Pin." Her voice cracked finally. "We just want to talk to you. *Please.*"

Pregnant women don't get rebuffed, even by street level graffiti artists.

We stood slightly awkwardly in her tiny kitchen while she made us all tea. "I don't know what I can tell you," she said. Her words were measured, considered in advance. Nothing wasted. Eager to manage expectations from the outset. "I only ever spoke to Samantha once. The police talked to me about it."

"I didn't know that," Alison said.

"Kayleigh," Mojo Pin said after a moment's hesitation. "My name is Kayleigh."

Something about knowing her name brought the air back into the room. Suddenly she was just a woman. We'd brought our own expectations up the motorway with us, but the graffiti and all the rest of it was just something she did after the working day was over. It didn't define her.

"She just wanted advice," Kayleigh said. "Something happened to her that she couldn't explain and eventually she found me."

"How did she do that?" Alison asked.

"The same way everyone else does. *Online.*" She said it like a quiet accusation towards us. "Message boards. You can find me if you know what you're looking for and you're really tenacious. Which your daughter *most certainly* was."

Kayleigh paused to consider the both of us and, satisfied, she said: "Come to the other room. I suppose I can show you something."

Even knowing what to expect, the room from the picture was slightly startling. The graffiti on each of the four walls was almost completely concealed by the ephemera pinned to them. Two of the walls were covered with sections of Ordnance Survey maps, then pinned in various locations, and twine used to connect them. A wall was given over to yellow Post-It notes, each one scrawled with some historical or geographical information. Some of them contained the kernel of an idea for a phrase that would be found on a building somewhere and then tagged Mojo Pin. There was a battered old desk in the corner with a laptop and an angle-poise lamp. Notebooks and scrapbooks, overflowing with newspaper clippings and letters and photographs of locations, spilled across the surface.

"I can show you Samantha's message, if you want," Kayleigh said.

Alison rallied her attention from the room to the computer screen. Kayleigh trawled through her inbox and then stepped aside for us to read it.

Hi Mojo Pin,

My name is Samantha Ackroyd. From what I've gathered from the message boards, you're the person I need to talk to about this. It's a long story but I'll try to keep it short. Bullet points if necessary.

I'm 16. I started seeing a boy called Daniel a couple of months ago. We didn't tell anyone about it. We just wanted it to be about us, you know?

Daniel wasn't like other boys. He was quiet, intense in a sort of gawky and endearing way, but really fiercely intelligent. He always had a book with him wherever he went. Always.

We'd go out walking and he would tell me about the dreams he'd been having about finding a place that was hidden until you knew how to look for it. He'd researched it and realised that he wasn't the only one. So he'd go out and try to find whatever it was he was looking for. I think in retrospect he never really thought of me as his girlfriend. I was just someone he felt he could confide in.

So we were out on Harmondsworth Moor one day and we'd been following this riverside path. It was a beautiful day even though it was winter. Somehow we'd managed to get as lost as you possibly can with the sound of traffic on the M25 and the planes in Heathrow thundering in your ears. We ended up in this heavily wooded area and it was when we got to a clearing in the centre that something changed. We could both feel it immediately. This POWER. This enormous fucking ENERGY in the area. It felt like we'd stuck our fingers in an electrical socket. I thought I was having a panic attack, but at the same time I felt this incredible sense of euphoria. Like doing ecstasy at a rave and losing all of your inhibitions. I looked at Daniel and suddenly I WANTED him. It was like a pure blast of teenage hormones. I wanted to drag him down into the leaves and just have him deep inside of me. But Daniel looked like he'd just discovered the meaning of life. His face took on this strange, distant quality. Like he was folding in on himself. I realise now that he'd finally found the place he'd been dreaming about. He wandered away, into the trees, like he was being called or led, and although I tried to follow him, it felt like I was moving through treacle.

And then he stopped, just ahead of me. Froze in his tracks for what seemed like ages, staring intently at something I couldn't really understand. It was like a sun made up of thousands of colours. Daniel looked over his shoulder then and just smiled. That fucking enigmatic smile he had that made me love him so much. And then he stepped forward and the colours seemed to take hold of him and swallow him up. It was as if he'd found a tear in the world that he couldn't resist, not even if it meant leaving everything else behind.

I started crying and laughing at the same time. I thought I was going to explode. Everything I felt was amplified, out of control. It was too much. I started to run after him but all the colours faded then. They sort of fizzled out to nothing. I waited. I wanted to stay as long as I could, in case he came back. But it got late and he didn't, so I left.

I didn't tell anyone about Daniel vanishing. I realise that it was a selfish thing to do. No one knew about our relationship so when his parents reported him missing, they didn't come to me at all.

And why did I do this? Because by the time I'd got home, all I wanted to do was go back to that wood and experience that incredible sensation again. And I realised that I NEEDED to go where Daniel had gone. More than anything else in the world. I wanted it to just be about me and him and that place.

I keep dreaming about it. I dream about changing and becoming something else. Escaping. I'm not religious. I don't believe in God or anything, but I read about the transfiguration of Jesus on Wikipedia the other day, and the line '...the meeting place of the temporal and the eternal', really struck a chord with me. I think this is what I've been dreaming of. Maybe.

But I can't find it anymore.

I've been back again and again and it's not where it was. Or maybe I've got the location all wrong. I feel like I'm going round in circles, getting more and more desperate. I feel like I'm changing, but I'm trapped between one place and the next. The place where Daniel went.

I know this probably sounds insane, and you're going to tell me to go to the police. But can you not do that and just help me?

"She left me her mobile number and asked me to call her," Kayleigh said. "And I *did* tell her to go to the police, but I think she was too far gone at that point. I've seen it happen before with people who are exposed to these places."

"What are we talking about here?" I said. "This place Samantha and Daniel stumbled on."

Kayleigh sighed. I think she'd danced around this subject for so long with so many people online that it almost felt like a chore to spell it out to us. She led us to the wall covered with pieces of OS maps, and pointed to the places marked with larger and larger circles radiating from central locus points in the landscape. Some of them were situated in these edge-lands, these forgotten little pockets between the city and the countryside, but others were deep inside cities, where legions of people would pass by every day.

"OK, look, I'm going to explain this *once* to you, and you either listen to me and take it on board, or you can leave. It's probably going to sound insane to you. I understand that reaction. If you're new to this sort of thing, it can make people like me sound like the tin-foil hat brigade. But remember that *you* asked, and this was what I told Samantha. OK?"

"OK," Alison said.

"This kind of place that Samantha and her boyfriend encountered can be found all over the land. Not just here, but everywhere. Some people call them blisters in space-time. Sometimes they're crossing points that people pass through – Roman roads, ley-lines; places that are like palimpsests of memory – but they can occur anywhere. They erupt up out of the landscape. They're loaded with meaning, atmosphere, symbols. They do something to our consciousness when we approach them."

"So how does that work if thousands of people pass through?" I asked. "They don't all disappear like Daniel."

"No, of course not. These liminal points affect people in different ways. Sometimes they exert their influence in tiny, almost insignificant respects; changing the way we walk to work, subtly altering how we feel about things, setting off conversations we might have, sparking memories that we might have thought lost. Sometimes we might see something from that spot in our mind, some fragment of its history..."

"And sometimes we disappear into thin air," I said.

"Sometimes it requires a purity of purpose. It's all individual. Someone might come to that place with all of this knowledge and every intention of enlightenment, and receive nothing substantial because there's a sort of cynical attitude to that approach too."

"Why did you send her to Alan Fletcher?" Alison said. There was a brittle sound to her voice that happened whenever his name came up. I reached for her hand, but she didn't want contact at that point.

"I don't know what it is you think you know about Alan, but he didn't have anything to do with Samantha's death. The police talked to him and released him."

"He'd been *sectioned* for months prior to this."

"Look, I understand. You're a Mum. I *get* it. I *do*. Nothing is enough when you can't bring the picture into focus. But I sent her to Alan because he experienced something similar, and it sent him spiralling away from the world he knew and understood, and left him with something some people might consider far more enriching."

"It sent him mad!"

"Alan isn't mad," Kayleigh said. "Not really. After what he experienced, he finally saw the world for what it was, and that life he'd lived suddenly seemed like a pale reflection of what it could be."

❖

I purposely didn't do anything more than redecorate the room we'd earmarked for the baby's nursery until the second scan, at 21 weeks. This is sometimes called the anomaly scan. We left the house early that morning. Autumn was a starting to make its presence felt. Leaves scattered across the quiet streets, a chill in the air, and a palpable change in the mood of the city.

We'd emptied the room a few weeks ago, and I'd stripped off the wallpaper, redecorated in a neutral colour, laid new carpet. When the sun rose in the morning, the room was flooded with light. There was the growing awareness that part of my life was ending, giving way to something else, a hitherto unexplored avenue that I'd nonetheless always known was there. The *nesting instinct*. For Alison it was a far more complex journey to navigate. Two becoming three was something she'd done before, then three to two and back to one again. The loneliest number. Life wasn't supposed to work that way. It fucks with your internal wiring. So we felt our way forward, tentatively, together.

I'd found myself sleeping less, plagued by dreams of a kid looking to lose himself in a fold in the world, and another left abandoned by the side of the road. I wanted to know what had happened to them. I wanted Alison to have some kind of resolution. I wanted *Samantha* to have resolution. Without that I didn't think we could move forward in any legitimate, meaningful sense. So I stood in this empty room, waiting for the sun to rise, and I wondered if I could slip inside the realness of its good intentions, its hopes for the future and the life of my child.

We found ourselves in the same little room with the same woman from nine weeks ago. The same scene, played out with tiny distinctions. We were still holding our breath, aware of how vulnerable life is in these little moments. Everything can change. I kissed Alison's forehead as Kerry listed our unborn child's body parts, all in good order. When she turned the monitor around I knew we were in the clear, and I felt a sweet rush of elation. It only led me back to Samantha though, out there at the nexus point, hysterical with all of her emotions pushed to eleven.

"Do you want to find out baby's sex today?" Kerry asked. We glanced at each other, even though we'd already discussed it.

"No, we'd like to wait and let it be a surprise," Alison said and squeezed my hand tightly. Another rush of emotion, a wave of love so pure and unsullied by anything that I felt my eyes brimming with tears.

I looked at the sea of black and silver and saw our child then: fingers and feet and nose and knees. And that underwater heartbeat, loud and strong.

"You have a very happy, healthy baby," Kerry said. "Would you like a photo?"

I still have it folded in my wallet. I look at it every now and then, all this time later, when I want to see what I lost.

We found Alan Fletcher a couple of weeks later, after some discussion. Alison still harboured her doubts about him, and I understood that, but I argued that we still needed the final piece of the puzzle in order to really make some kind of informed opinion about Samantha's death.

"If you're going to be all fucking articulate and reasonable about things, then I have *no* idea what I'm bringing to this relationship anymore," Alison said.

It only took a couple of hours of diligent searching in the area around Heathrow to find the man. He had a grubby little caravan buried in the shadow of the M25. When we got out of the car, I said "Benefit of the doubt, remember?" to Alison. She nodded, her face suddenly very sober, very determined, and so very, very sad. I hated it when I got home from work on a dark afternoon and found her looking like that. Bereft. No one wants to see that in the face of the person they love. I tried hard to chase that pain from her eyes. I don't know whether I succeeded or not. But I tried.

Fletcher wasn't in when we knocked, but we didn't have to wait long for him to come home. The sun was falling below the horizon when he emerged from some woods on the western side of the motorway. We'd become accustomed to the constant roar of traffic above us.

I think part of me sensed immediately that something about Fletcher was off, but I didn't see it there and then. He had his head bowed with the exhaustion of another day of walking under his belt. Long hair tied back into a ponytail, a really out of control beard, streaked with white and black and grey. A Berghaus waterproof jacket and some Salomon Quest hiking boots were the only obvious concessions to a moneyed past. Later I'd note the scuffed face of a Rolex watch on his wrist, the iPad Pro, and the Montblanc fountain pen. These were just remnants of the man he'd once been. Little else remained.

But it wasn't any of that that stopped us in our tracks when Fletcher finally glanced up. It was something alien, something too slippery to grasp immediately. All of the colour was *gone* from him. I don't mean he was pale or sick; I mean he was black and white with shades of grey. Like old newspaper print. The closer he came, the clearer and stranger it became.

"Alan Fletcher?" I said as I crossed the overgrown patch of scrubland where his caravan was pitched. I tried to say more, but his condition had left me almost speechless.

He looked alarmed, slightly bewildered. I wondered if he was on medication or flying without chemical support entirely. He froze, his rucksack falling from his shoulders when he saw Alison behind me. He stared at her bump, his mouth falling open. He seemed to be muttering something to himself.

"We just want to talk to you, Alan," I said levelly, raising my hands. "We don't want any trouble. We're alone."

"We've seen Mojo Pin," Alison said, her voice steadier than I expected it to be. "*Kayleigh.*"

I saw something dawn in Fletcher's eyes then, and the ghost of a smile trembled on his grey lips. He glanced around, looking slightly surprised to find himself outside his caravan. "Where are my manners," he said finally. A deep voice; all received pronunciation, as if he was a BBC news presenter. "If you know Kayleigh, you must come inside and I'll put the kettle on." He picked up his rucksack and unlocked the door, glanced back at us. "*Come on*, then…"

There wasn't much room to sit inside the caravan. Eventually after some manoeuvring, Fletcher realised how uncomfortable we were and moved a great swathe of maps and books from the dining table and bench so we could sit. We stared at him, trying to grasp the nature of his condition. His clothes had been bleached of colour too. He looked like someone had cut out his picture from a newspaper and glued it onto the world, with all its profusion of colours. He seemed blissfully unaware of the affliction, or perhaps it had been long enough for him to forget how he appeared to others. When he put the mugs of tea on the table before us, he said, "You're Samantha's mother aren't you?"

Alison looked at him across the table, seeing beyond the oddity of his condition for the moment. "Yes."

"I expect you must be quite confused about the nature of your daughter's death." He rubbed at his scalp nervously. "I hope you don't think I'm responsible in any way."

"That's why we're here," I said. "I think we'd both like some clarification about what happened to Samantha."

"Are you her father?"

"No," I said.

"No, I didn't think so. She mentioned him being absent for most of her life. Didn't sound like he'd care much now."

"What did you talk to Samantha about?" Alison asked.

"Oh, a great many things," Fletcher said. "She was a *lovely*, bright girl. She told me about her boyfriend vanishing one day on Harmondsworth Moor. Kayleigh had said that I could explain what had most likely happened to him. Of course, I couldn't give her a *definitive* answer, but I could give her my best guess, based on a fair bit of field work, you know; *deep* topographical exploration."

"What happened to Daniel?" I asked. "In your opinion."

Fletcher rooted through a pile of OS maps and a landslide of old, musty smelling hardbacks at his feet. He unfolded one of the maps that covered the local regions. There were marks made in various locations, speculative lines drawn from one point to another. "These places, based on my research, are what we like to refer to as liminal points."

"Kayleigh explained them to us," Alison said. "She said they were like blisters in space-time."

"Yes, perhaps they are. It's where these maps deepen into more than just lines on paper. If we look *hard* enough, or we come to these places with enough *intent* or purity, they can afford us a glimpse of somewhere else, *something* else."

"But Daniel just vanished," Alison said.

"Yes, well, I've tried to ascertain some of the boy's story. Obviously there must be something in his background that primed him for this extraordinary occurrence. That sort of event doesn't just happen by chance."

"What did Samantha want?" Alison said. "What did she intend to do?"

"You must understand that when I met her in that cafe in Harmondsworth village, I told her from the outset: go home, go to your GP, and get some counselling. And when you're old enough, travel, work it from your system." Fletcher's face softened, and the clouds seemed to part in his eyes for a moment of clarity. "I have two sons. They're gone now. Their mother took them abroad, as far away from me as she could get. I've lost enough to be aware that my only real role that day was to dissuade Samantha from the path she'd decided she was on."

"But that didn't work, did it?" Alison wasn't accusing him. The statement came out sounding defeated.

"She already knew enough, felt enough not to be talked out of the course she was on. She'd started *dreaming* about it. She'd been exposed to the sheer power of one of these liminal points. It's like sailing too close to the sun. Like being tattooed. You can never dig out that place where it's touched you."

"Is that what it's done to you?" I asked. The elephant in the room. It had to be addressed sooner or later.

"This?" Fletcher shrugged. "Of course. This development occurred quite recently. I've spent too long trying to get *inside*. I'd sensed the presence of these places since childhood, I suppose. I'd be walking home from school, no more than a mile from here, and have these visions and reveries of the world changing in certain lights, certain times of the day. They were like glimpses of the *divine*. Something was woven into those days that

I suppose I'll never be able to fully explain. These transfigurations of the mundane give us little glimpses into something beyond what we can fully grasp, or articulate to someone else. I experienced it again a couple of years ago, but it was different this time. I was at a site we were in the process of buying for development, and I finally saw it for what it was: a beautiful piece of this countryside, being ripped up so we could build another *fucking* runway on the edge of Heathrow.

"I'd been enticed by something in the light that afternoon. Before I knew it I was on my own in a clearing. It was a miraculously hot day. Early May. It had just rained. A warm shower. I was soaked to the skin. The sun seemed to capture everything in its rays for a fleeting moment. The sound of the traffic receded, the planes; all of it. I realised that it was the viaduct over a river I'd fished in as a child with my dad. Everything stopped then. The world, I mean. And there it was, just for a few seconds, this extraordinary moment of clarity. That I was being afforded a glimpse of what it was all for; that there was a greater purpose to life other than simply living it. I felt this extraordinary *elation*. That finally – finally! – I could be the man I'd always suspected I could be. It had nothing to do with family, or work, or possessions."

"But this," I said. "Is *this* really what you wanted for yourself?" It sounded cruel but I just wanted to know.

"*This* is just temporary. Unfortunately the body still requires rest and sustenance. There's nothing I can do about that. But soon, I won't need this body at all."

"You won't need your *body*?" Alison said.

"I'm in transition. This body is gradually being discarded. I've done a lot of walking in this past year. Staines, Stanwell Moor, Harmondsworth Moor, Thorney Park golf course, Heathrow Terminal 5. I've wandered into Holiday Inns, Hiltons and Travelodges and then been escorted right out again. I've followed the river Colne, investigated care homes and petrol stations and nature reserves. My ambition is to hold this entire region in my mind so I *become* the region. This is the extent of my spiritual ambition."

Fletcher was nodding emphatically as he gathered momentum. Confusion and lucidity at war within him. "Of course, Samantha is already there."

"What do you mean, she's already there?" Alison said. It was as if someone had plugged her into an electrical socket. "My daughter is fucking *dead*."

"Her body may be dead but I believe she's everywhere now," Fletcher said. "*Everywhere*. She *understood* it instinctively. I could tell within minutes of talking to her. She'd been born with that seed of something in her that wanted more. And of course, she'd lost the first boy she'd ever loved. Of *course* she'd get there first. There's something to be said about purity of purpose; it cuts through all this abstruse language and gets right to the *heart* of it all."

Alison looked at me helplessly. What did you do with that kind of information? How did it help? The longer we lingered with Fletcher, the more fractured his attention became. He said kids came and threw stones at him and the caravan. He told me about a place close to here where countless histories crossed and lay buried beneath the ground. The endless narrative of nature and humanity. Things that had fallen but with our help could rise again in our minds. I wasn't clear whether this was another doorway to the divine, or a dead end. But that was where it began for me. Just as Alison was getting ready to leave, I saw it in Fletcher's eyes. I saw myself reflected back at me, lost in the viaducts of Fletcher's dream. It was like a tattoo. You could never properly dig it out of your skin.

We were waiting to hear the now familiar burst of amplified heartbeat from the scanner, but there was just this tense extended silence. I could hear my heart again, fit to burst right out of my chest. Alison's hand clutching mine tightly. *Don't let this happen. Don't let this happen.* Finally Kerry put down her equipment and said, "I'm sorry."

I felt the room lurch away from me. There was a crib and a pram waiting at home. We were *prepared* for our child now. Those rooms were going to be a home again. Kerry went to fetch a midwife. The subsequent hours blurred around us. There was a leaflet handed to me about the medical management of late miscarriages. The doctor finally signed a prescription for a tablet to trigger the process that would lead, 48 hours later, to labour. We spent two days walking around the house with our dead baby already haunting us. I don't remember that time very well. Just quiet, desperate dismay. How could this happen to two people who'd already had more than their fair share of grief? How was this, in any possible fucking way, *fair?*

When we returned to the hospital the midwife led us to an office used for bereaved families. After a while we were ushered into a labour suite for the first of a sequence of internal examinations. The labour took most of the day. There was a break and I excused myself to go the toilet. Instead I went outside and cried. Great gasping sobs. A couple passing by gave me a wide berth. After a moment, I composed myself and went back inside. Alison, after all, didn't have the same luxury of excusing herself.

We saw the baby very briefly, still in its amniotic sac. The midwife placed her in a basket with a white blanket. She was very small, very perfect. For a moment I fooled myself that this was all a mistake, that our baby was here in the world, ready to take home. But no. She was an assemblage of tiny fingers and toes, eyes shut tight, her heart forever still. Our poor dead daughter.

Afterwards I faced the interminable tangle of paperwork covering the funeral and post-mortem arrangements. We finally left the hospital after midnight. We drove home in silence – there were no words. After I'd put an exhausted Alison to bed I went upstairs to the nursery. It still smelled of fresh paint. The crib in flat-pack form. The light was gone from the room. Even when the morning came, nothing would reach it.

There was a panoply of emotions to navigate. Emptiness was the strongest. A long flat despondency that refused your requests for egress. Sadness and anger and guilt and fatigue would come later. I boxed my feelings up and placed them where I would have no easy access to them. Society has groomed men not to talk about these things, to disconnect. I felt like I'd gone quietly mad.

I'd started dreaming of a map marking all of the liminal points. I dreamed about a kaleidoscope of colour enfolding me, leading me to uncharted territories. I dreamed about my daughter becoming a larva in the process of transformation. Strange events happening under the surface. Everything being redistributed, recycled, reformed; an old shape ready to be shrugged off so that something new and glorious could take its place. I woke bereft, tears drying on my face.

I found Alison upstairs one day, running her hands over the baby clothes. A tactile way to bring the bruise to the surface, to access something in this absence. I didn't know how to *act* around her. Should I be strong, or optimistic, or should I just hold onto her, to show that I was there to weather this storm with her?

"How do I fix this?" I asked one night, in desperation. "How do I make it better?"

"You *can't*," she said. "You just can't."

Three weeks later Alison packed a bag and flew to Rome for a photo-shoot. She assured me she was OK, that when she got back we'd talk about our future. I felt my insides knotting.

I hung around the house for the first day, and then I went out and found myself in Alan Fletcher's edge-lands, looking for something I couldn't define. I walked in his steps for a couple of days, across the bastard countryside. I went to the lonely spot by the side of Junction 15 of the M25, where they'd found Samantha's body. Solemn ribbons of concrete off-ramps sprawling above me, the roar of traffic and planes taking off and landing. There was nothing to find there, just a grass verge, cars flying past. I had no idea where the exact spot was that they'd discovered her. But I hoped that some part of her still existed here, just as Fletcher had suggested, transfigured into the landscape. I closed my eyes and sent out a request for her to guide me.

I drifted then for three days and nights. I crossed allotments and camping grounds, landfill and woodlands, golf courses, Terminal 5, walked past executive homes with double garages. I slept rough and badly, waking shivering in the middle of the night in my sleeping bag. It felt like an ordeal I had to pass through to find the other side, to feel the map deepening into more than lines on paper. Parts of me unravelling gradually, falling away until the raw nerves were exposed. But there was something else beneath all that.

I was mad by the end of it, somehow purged of the emptiness I felt, and it was then that I found what I was looking for. I was crossing the river Colne by way of a pretty little bridge on Cricketfield Road when it happened. I was exhausted, a sack of bones slouching through the landscape, when the hours fell away from me and became nothing. In the failing light of the evening the world changed shape and the back of my mind began to itch with a sensation beyond description. It was made up of joy and adrenaline, tears and yearning. I clutched at the rails of the bridge but they turned to mist in my hands. There was a parting, a shifting, a moment where space and time aligned perfectly. It was a new way of seeing through the world, through layers of meaning and the wisdom of millennia of human narrative to what was always there, waiting for us all. A *deeper* secret. The pearl in the flesh of the oyster. But even revealed it gave way to more profound mysteries.

I stood there, awed. All the colours of the world bled away then came back with such extraordinary vitality that I wept at the sight of it. The air was hot and scented and golden. I was at the *confluence*. All the atoms in the universe straining to be in alignment. In that moment I wanted only to live inside it, to discard this tired old body and take my place in its harmony and perfection. To cross over or be transfigured. It would be so *easy*. I'd be spared the heartache and uncertainty of old age, encroaching disease and the inevitable indignity of death. My Get-Out-Of-Jail card. I began to step forward, laughing.

Then I heard the sound, and felt an ugly vibration in my pocket. I glanced down, momentarily mystified at the unfamiliar shape of my body. I'd already partially forgotten what it was for. The sound persisted. I tried to step away from it, but I couldn't. *My phone is ringing*, some distant part of me said. My tether. I saw Alison's face then, saw the empty rooms we'd both walked away from. But empty rooms are not your life.

I felt the gravity of it all calling me back, away from this gently insidious madness, back to the world I knew; the one made out of lost children and shattered hearts. *Come back*, it said. *We're not done with you yet.*

Alison was calling from Ciampino Airport to tell me she was waiting for her flight home. She wanted me to pick her up from Heathrow when she landed. I was bewildered, shaken by my experience, still caught between two worlds. I had enough time to get a train home and shower and throw my clothes into the laundry. Later I waited at the airport, grasping at the memory of what had happened, trying to decide if it had changed me. The first thing Alison wanted to know was what had happened to my hair. It was streaked with grey. Later we discovered that shards of grey had also lodged themselves in the blue of my eyes. I suppose it was a small price to pay for flying too close to the sun.

But something else had changed in that distance of four days. We began to talk on the way home. It was delicate. We were like Bambi on ice for weeks afterward, but we were aware that some of the immediate pain had healed. We were being lifted away from the quiet dismay of our lives since the miscarriage. We made tentative plans that suggested we'd survived and we were going to be able to move on. We talked about selling the house and getting out of the city. I joked that Alison had only needed to be alone and to think carefully about the future. I'd had to go on a solitary dream-quest, sleeping rough and going mad. Typical male response. She didn't laugh. I suppose it wasn't all that funny.

And then one afternoon I came home and I found Alison upstairs in what would have been the nursery. The sun was gradually finding its way back in. She'd opened the windows. After a moment she said, "It's just an empty room again."

"Is it?" I said, taking her hand.

She looked at me and nodded.

We got married one cold morning in December. It was a dark and stormy day. Just me and Alison and a few friends at a register office. We said our lines and we kissed and then it was over. We stood on the street afterwards with confetti in our hair, laughing. That same day, Alan Fletcher's body was found outside a scrap metal yard in Staines. I didn't tell Alison. It didn't feel like part of our lives moving forward. But I imagined him standing at that precipice, awed at all the secret colours of the world, aware that there was nothing remaining to call him back. And so he left his earthly body behind gladly, and he took his place in all that harmony and perfection. Suddenly he was everywhere.

Everywhere.

Oathkeeper

Maura McHugh

The storm had not yet arrived, but towering, smoky-violet thunderheads were its bannermen. They marched from deep in the Atlantic and dragged behind them huge white-capped waves fringing a cloak of churning darkness.

Standing in the deserted car park beside Ballytrae harbour, Douglas felt their approaching menace in his bones.

He turned to his wife. "We've missed the ferry Ríona. Or it's been cancelled. Let's get a B&B and hunker down before that bastard hits."

She looked up at him, winked, and he spotted she had her mobile phone at her ear. "We're here," she said into it.

A fast spatter of icy rain hit, and Douglas winced. He pulled up his raincoat's hood and fastened all the buttons so only his long face was visible. He turned his back and hunched against the squall. The straps of his rucksack dug into his shoulders.

"I see you," Ríona said. She took off at a brisk pace down the short sloping road toward the twin stone piers spearing into the horseshoe-shaped bay. She gestured at Douglas to follow.

He broke into a half jog to catch up. Ríona was petite but had a Jack Russell's energy and determination. Nothing ever prevented her getting her way, and Douglas spent most of their relationship running to keep up with her despite being a foot taller.

A small fishing boat with a bright lamp and a chugging engine pulled up to the farthest pier. A shimmering blue shark was painted across the top of its small white cabin, and over it the words *Siorc Gorm*. A hulking man kitted out in heavyweight rain gear and wellies threw a loop of encrusted rope over a rusty iron bollard embedded in the pier, pulling it tight in seconds. He called a greeting and held out a hand. Ríona grasped it before jumping down into the boat and giving the man a hug around his waist.

Huffing up, Douglas noticed the slick surface of the deck, and was glad to take the steadfast grip of the stranger. Despite the aid his feet skidded slightly as he landed and Douglas half-fell into the large man, who stank of fish and seaweed. Douglas got the impression of a deeply-tanned, lined face and bristly white whiskers under his concealing hood.

The wind was picking up so Ríona raised her voice. "Doug, this is Bradán. He'll take us to the Island."

"Bout ye big lad," Bradán said in a guff voice.

"Hello—" but that's all Douglas could manage, as Ríona was already removing the line, and Bradán had ducked back into the cabin to engage the engine.

Ríona handed Douglas an orange life jacket, and he followed her into the cabin – it was a snug fit with the three of them. Ríona helped Douglas extricate himself from his rucksack and struggle into the life jacket. By the time he and Ríona were sorted the boat was pushing through the choppy grey waves outside the small bay and heading swiftly to the mostly northerly island off the coast of Antrim. The wipers on the windows worked steadily to keep them clear of the hard rain knocking against the panes.

Douglas risked a look to the west, where the massed clouds obscured the setting sun, and his heartbeat jumped several pulses.

Ríona must have noticed his expression because she grabbed his hand and gave it a squeeze. "It's not as close as it looks," she said.

She pointed ahead to the outline of the Island. Jutting out from its rocky peak the pale obelisk of the lighthouse was imprinted on the gloom. Its warning light spun sedately, the last marker of humanity before the Arctic.

"My family were the Keepers from when it was first built in 1869 until it was automated in 1991. The fishermen hereabouts call it The Last Light."

She lowered her voice slightly, so she was barely audible over the engine. "Of course, the Scots really have that honour, but..." she smiled and shrugged as if that explained local pride.

Douglas gripped the handles set into the cabin walls and tried not to pay attention to his lurching stomach. It wasn't so much the up and down motion that disturbed him, but the deep rolls from side to side. He licked his lips and tasted salt. He reached down carefully and dug a cannister of water from a mesh pouch on the outside of his rucksack.

He swallowed a couple of mouthfuls, and focused on the approaching island, a steady point in the moving tableau of roiling ocean and boiling clouds.

Ríona stood close to Bradán and spoke quickly and quietly to him. Douglas couldn't concentrate on what they were saying due to his nausea, and the noise of the engine, wind and the rain. Douglas hated to admit it, but he found the Northern Irish accent impenetrable at times: its unfamiliar cadence, unusual slang and the rapid-fire delivery made him feel dim-witted as his brain laboured to deliver delayed catch-up of every sentence's meaning. Their first night in Belfast had left him feeling permanently drunk – although a lot of Bushmills had been consumed.

Back in her homeland, Ríona's accent had deepened to the point that Douglas had to ask her to repeat herself a few times. It was the first time that he'd visited *Norn Iron* (as she called it) since their whirlwind romance and marriage. None of her family, the Dunnes, had attended their simple wedding ceremony at Islington Town Hall in London. It had been his mother and brother, and their assorted friends: his rather conservative accounting colleagues, and her outrageously colourful gaggle of comedians, drag kings and queens, actors and artists.

"You are my bold heart," he'd said, and slipped the ring on her finger.

"You are my North Star," she'd said as they bound themselves together.

Since the wedding they had nested together well, their attraction and love deepening with time rather than numbing under the dull weight of routine. Ríona prodded his rather serious nature into action and adventure, and he steadied her when her flighty spirit burst into overwrought intensity.

As an apology for not being able to attend the ceremony, the Dunnes had sent a carefully packaged pen and ink illustration of the lighthouse on the Island, blotted about with inky clouds and ragged waves crashing upon its shining resolve.

A fluid copperplate inscription titled it 'Oathkeeper'.

Ríona cried when she unwrapped it, and sat, bent-headed, with it on her lap for some minutes. Then she hung it in a shadowed corner of their flat, which he thought was odd, until he got up one night to visit the loo and realised the moon shone directly upon it. The tower *glimmered*. The spark in the lantern pulsed.

He froze, his toes cold against the carpet in the hallway, his bladder suddenly more urgent. It did not comfort him, as he imagined blind ships on chaotic seas would feel at sighting its beacon. He felt *warned*.

He inched forward and flicked on the light switch. Under the glare of electricity the drawing flattened into an ordinary image. From that point on Douglas never walked through that passage at night without a light on. Yet sometimes he sensed a glint under the covering glare, a disquieting watchfulness.

Ríona had promised that they would visit her family for a late honeymoon, but it had taken another year before they could arrange enough time off to book a proper holiday, since their respective jobs had different periods of busyness. Their free time remained out of synch until an abrupt alignment last weekend when

Ríona's show was cancelled, due to the venue going out of business with no notice.

Dipping and cresting over waves, chased by a storm as they sped to an isolated island facing the dead space north of the Atlantic, Douglas figured this was a mite too far into his discomfort zone.

He was about to say something when Bradán spun the wheel hard, and the ship lurched. Douglas closed his eyes, gripped the bar tight, and tasted stomach acid in his mouth.

Bradán laughed and shouted, "Dead-on! Still got it wee lass."

Douglas opened his eyes when the wind and horizontal rain buffeted him from the open cabin door. It sounded like a jet engine was blasting toward them. Bradán was a dark shape on the deck, casting his lines from the prow and aft onto bollards sticking like spikes out of a pier that was cut out of the island's rockface. The boat's plastic fenders squealed as it surged against the wall with the waves. Bradán lowered a short gangway to the pier and to Douglas's horror, Ríona ran across it nimbly. She carried a heavyweight torch in one hand and her rucksack in her other.

Bradán turned to him. "Get across quick ya big lump."

Pure terror locked his limbs when he watched the tiny metal bridge moving up and down. Rain and spray lashed his face. Across what seemed like a raging gorge, his wife shouted encouragements, even though the storm whipped away the exact words.

A large hand clamped upon the neck of his coat and he was half lifted, half flung across to the Island.

He landed and managed to stay upright due to a gust of wind hitting him with a counter-balancing force.

Ríona grabbed him and stared up at his face intently. "I've got you!" she yelled above the gale. She thumped him on the back, turned and quickly threw the lines back to the *Siorc Gorm*, bucking on the waves. The gangway was already retracted.

"What?" Douglas shouted, stunned, as Bradán steered the boat out of the harbour, and with it the main light that illuminated the area bobbed away into the maelstrom.

"My rucksack!" He'd left it in the cabin. Fear and frustration crashed in his chest.

His wife raised her torch and turned it on. A bright spotlight, shredded through by torrential rain, illuminated the steps carved into the stone – thankfully there was a strong metal railing alongside.

"Ach, get on love," Ríona said. The manic grin on her face indicated she was thriving on the drama of the event. "Fret not, I've spare kex in my bag." She pushed her rucksack into his arms, and he slung the bag over a shoulder, astonished at its weight. Once again, he was suffused with admiration for his indominable woman.

She led the way, directing the torch with her left hand and holding onto the metal railing with her right. The wind alternatively punched or pushed them during their steep ascent so it was slow, careful going. The sheer force of the rain prevented Douglas from looking at the approaching storm directly, but from his water-logged periphery it was a roaring maw.

At the top of the steps the guide rail continued a short

distance to a long white-washed building. A light shone in one of its small square windows, deep-set, indicating thick walls. The Keeper's Quarters. Relief washed through him.

They huddled at the red wooden door while Ríona rummaged for the key. Douglas glanced up at the immense bleached tower looming above and the moving beam of light strafing the rain. That same *frisson* he felt in his hallway hit him again but multiplied a thousand-fold. For a frightful moment he was more petrified of this alien place than the devouring tempest rushing upon them.

Ríona produced an old-fashioned iron key with an elaborately knotted head. She raised it and kissed the metal with her eyes closed. She waited a beat before inserting it into the lock. It turned – dispelling the sudden fear that seized Douglas that they could be stranded without shelter.

The immediacy of their precarious situation diminished once they entered the house and pressed the door closed on the storm's entreaties.

For an extended moment they leaned their backs against the door, and as one released a shuddering breath. After the madness outside it was like entering a sanctuary. Water sluiced off their clothing. Douglas became aware he was soaked to his skin, despite a sturdy raincoat. The weather had changed dramatically while they were en route to Ballytrea, so he hadn't been wearing the correct kit for a full-on Atlantic outrage.

He stepped out of the short hallway and peered to the left of the long room. A square table was surrounded by a cushioned bench on three sides. Each white wall was punctured by a small thick-paned window. Well-worn rugs covered the slate floor. Ahead, a fire frolicked in a wood-burning stove, and next to it lay a big pile of logs. On the right was the compact kitchen, and after that a hall that stretched past three doors towards an arched doorway. The electric lights were on, but no one was visible.

He turned back and started at the sight of Ríona stripped down to her bra and pants. The smile began automatically before the logical part of his brain interjected about the probability of company.

"Isn't your family here?" he whispered in a shocked tone.

"I'm saturated, and not going to drip all over the house." She hung up her life jacket, coat, top and jeans on strategically placed hangers. Her boots were already sitting in a shoe rack. He twigged that this problem must be a regular occurrence in this place, and perhaps the reason for the hallway. A curtain rail hung over the end, with a heavy curtain tied off to one side. But there were no other coats or shoes.

She picked up her rucksack and padded into the kitchen. "I'm gagging for a cuppa tae," she said. The wind moaned down the chimney, as if in agreement.

Outside the storm mauled the island, but in this refuge it was a distant tantrum.

Quickly, nervously, Douglas followed her lead and undressed until he was down to his trunks. He stepped cautiously into the room. Ríona already had the kettle on the stove and a teapot ready. She had located an oversized robe and slippers, and looked like a child wearing an adult's clothing. That idea cooled his ardour somewhat.

She pointed to the hallway. "Root around in the first bedroom. You'll find clothes." She continued opening cabinets and the fridge, assessing stock.

The lights flickered and dimmed. They both froze. Ríona touched one of the walls.

Quietly: "Hold it together lass."

The power surged back to full strength. And she nodded as if satisfied.

Douglas walked into the first bedroom: it had a double bed with a quilt sitting on top of several layers of blankets. Ríona had unceremoniously dumped the contents of her bag onto the bed – he sighed. His wife was not the neatest of people, but he resisted his urge to begin sorting through and tidying it away. Miraculously, most of it was dry, and she hadn't been joking about having spares of his underwear.

A large wooden wardrobe filled a niche. It protested on opening, and smelled musty. There were a variety of jumpers, hoodies, and pyjama bottoms in neat piles on the side shelves, thick socks in rolls in a drawer, and a long plaid robe on a hanger. He picked out a hodgepodge of clashing colours and patterns. Everything seemed big enough for a giant – or perhaps Bradán.

A neat stack of towels sat on a chair beside a side table with a lamp.

Warm and dry, he stepped into the hallway and glanced to the left. The next two doors were shut. A little tile hung on the farthest door with the words "The Jacks" and a cartoon image of a toilet.

He stood in front of the middle door and raised his hand to knock. For some reason he sensed disapproval about the action. He faltered, unsure, afraid of disturbing someone in a space that didn't belong to him.

In the kitchen the kettle whistled a beckoning song, so he retreated to his wife.

She had half a digestive biscuit sticking out of her mouth. She pointed at the table and mumbled something that Douglas took to be instructions to sit down. He did so, and ran his palms across the old wood, deeply varnished and notched with history. He imagined generations of the Dunne family sitting at this table, eating, laughing and working to keep the lighthouse operating in defiance of the great ocean's whims.

The house shuddered, the lights flickered again, and Ríona was at his side plonking a tray down on the table. On it sat a teapot in a crocheted cosy, two mugs, a jug of milk, a plate of biscuits and a bottle of Black Bush whiskey, three quarters full.

He eyed the bottle and glanced at his wife. "Did you get a head start, woman?"

She poured tea into the mugs and said primly, "The early bird sips first."

Ríona made the tea the way he liked, with only a suggestion of milk and no sugar, while hers was the opposite. Douglas felt the tension of the day dissipate under the magic of the most grounding, fundamental rituals of life.

They said nothing for a time, enjoying the break and listening to the aggrieved storm, cheated of its playthings. She poured a generous dollop of whiskey into their mugs once they were empty, and under the table she stroked his shins with a foot. Her smile was mischievous and knowing. He reached over and ran the tips of his fingers over her agile left hand and up her forearm. He felt something different: a series of bumps.

Douglas frowned. It felt like cartilage embedded under the skin. He caressed the area again to ensure he wasn't mistaken, and the protuberances *shifted*. He jerked his hand away in surprise.

BANG! BANG! BANG!

Douglas jumped. He looked at Ríona. She sat ramrod straight, with eyes closed and her face set in stoic lines.

"Here we go," she said.

"Nobody could be out in that, surely…" He trailed off at his wife's grimace.

She stood up and walked to the entranceway. Douglas got up but lingered inside the room.

The door opened and the fire *whoosed* and flared up from the gale that rushed in.

Ríona said something but the violence of the elements drowned it out.

The door shut again: cutting off the din.

Douglas stepped forward to peer into the hallway.

Ríona stood alone. A black harpoon, long and with a vicious curved hook, leaned against their coats, dripping water into a small puddle.

He waited for her to explain. Instead she looked desperately unhappy, her right hand rubbing her left forearm.

"Did UPS get lost?" he asked finally, jokey, but hearing the edge in his voice.

"Special delivery," she said, glum.

"Okay Ríona, what's going on? Where's your family." He pointed at the weapon. "What's this thing and how did it get here?"

"It's just us," she said. "No one's coming. Until later."

Outside a deafening roar reverberated through the very stone of the island and vibrated up their bones. It was a sound that the primal part of Douglas's brain recognised, and it provoked a fear in him so intense he almost pissed himself.

He dropped into a crouch on the slate floor, trembling, his arms covering his head instinctively. An overwhelming dread permeated him. His imagination projected a blizzard of images, as if an ancient switch had been tripped to play a jumbled, fear-drenched recording in his mind.

He saw the oldest foe from an antediluvian era, the great serpentine enemy, with needle-sprayed chitin skin and razor teeth. Birthed from chaos, swimming in entropy, it could not be vanquished, merely faced and opposed every few generations.

Douglas heard Ríona, as if from a distance. Her hands upon his face calmed him.

"I need you to help, Doug, *please*. I choose you because you're so steadfast, and kind, and dependable." She kissed his forehead and it was a benediction. The darkness and despair fled from her love.

He stood, feeling frail and vulnerable. The thing bellowed again, shaking the world, setting his heart racing. The generator failed and the lights blinked out. Only the fire offered light... the fire, and her skin.

Luminescent glyphs pulsed across her body. She was changing: an adaptation to the primal presence outside.

Ríona grabbed his hand. Her touch removed doubt and replaced it with a calm clarity. She led him through the darkened hallway and to the door to the middle room.

The door swung open at her touch, revealing only a chest with silver bands. When she approached they shone with a blinding light. She lifted the cover, and inside lay her armour.

Douglas helped dress her in the flexible, radiant layer that fitted her perfectly, despite her extra height, new ridges along her arms and spines erupting from her back. He looked up into her iridescent irises, a spectrum of shifting colours.

He touched her cheek, now scaled and resilient.

"You are my bold heart," he said.

"You are my north star," she whispered.

Douglas knew what to do.

He returned to the entrance and collected the harpoon.

She waited for him, and Douglas took a moment to appreciate her splendour.

It felt as if her best qualities had manifested into an unearthly physical configuration of transcendent glory. Tears slid down his face because this gift was not available to him, or to most people.

He handed her the weapon and at her grip it elongated and sprouted tiny barbs.

She threw back her head and issued a keening challenge.

The responding howl cracked the glass in the windows.

She walked to the arched oak door, the opening to the tower, and touched her weapon to its aged wood.

It shimmered and became a gateway to the void.

The fight lay below, as it always does.

She bounded through the portal.

Douglas felt the long fall through the coiling loops, the first piercing of flesh, and the eternal grievous wound.

He remained standing, waiting: her bridge back or a channel for obliteration.

Far above, the tower's purposeful light continued to spin as the ravening storm tore into the walls.

The beam would keep rotating, even as it fell.

I Will Tell You Seven-Oh

M.R. Carey

It was a dark and stormy night. The moon was up there somewhere, full and round like a silver shilling, but it couldn't be seen through all the ragged rifts of cloud that glided down the great sky river towards a still-distant dawn.

All these things had to be true, by the way. None of it was accidental, or unlooked-for. If it hadn't been dark, Unsung Jill would have been blind. If it hadn't been wet, Peter couldn't have come up out of the lake. If there had been no moon, Kel would have had no claws and Anna could not have danced.

We would none of us have been ready for the great fight that was to come.

Let us say, for the sake of argument, that we were seven. Seven would have been a goodly number, after all. Seven small figures (for Kel was not in his furry coat yet, and Unsung Jill can be any size she wishes) running up the hill toward the castle wall.

Toward Errencester, where twice times one hundred men at arms waited for us. And one mage. And one monster.

I'm lying, though. There were only six that came to the castle that night, and six were not enough.

It seems I've no more wit for tales than I have for tallies. We must go back a little, to get the sense of this. Then we'll push on.

"...and come to our village?" Dam Alice said. "And help us? Fight for us?"

"What, now?" I muttered. I was only halfway through my supper, and tired from a long day's hunting. I hadn't been listening properly to what the two men and one woman had been saying to me. I didn't know why they were here, standing at the mouth of my hole in the queasy twilight that was neither one thing nor another. Out of the three, it was only the woman I recognised, as a friend of my mother's in times long gone. They bothered me somewhat, but not enough to make me want to kill them and eat them.

"We asked if you would come," the big man said. Tall. Tall man. Not big like Kel is big, for he had little heft to him. His body was gaunt, and his skin pocked with old sores. His silver hair was sparse. "We're in desperate need."

"Are you, then?" I said, and bit into the bird again. It was a moorhen, I think. I had plucked out most of the feathers, but left the bones in to give it some crunch. I chewed the spiky mouthful hard. I don't really taste things any more, but the jagged ends of the bones stuck into my cheeks and the roof of my mouth, which was almost the same as eating something with spice to it. The wounds healed over as soon as they were made. I don't ever hurt for long.

"The new lord has done terrible things to us," the other man said. He was small, even shorter than the woman, and very wide in the body. His limbs were short and his head was large. His red hair and beard were so full it looked like someone had set his head on fire. There's a name for the kind of man he was, but I don't remember it. "He takes everything we've got, and anyone who protests is cut down by his soldiers."

"The old lord rode us hard," Dam Alice declared, "but he was careful not to kill the chicken because he wanted to keep having eggs to eat. Ebberlin is different. He's married a lady from across the water, a magician's get, and she brought him a dower of spell-found gold richer than dreams. He doesn't need us any more. And I think he means to end us."

"What's that to me?" I asked. And then, because it seemed like a question they were better able to answer, "What can you offer me?"

"A home," the big man said. "You left Cosham because you didn't feel welcome there."

"True, yes. Very true. Pitchforks were stuck in me. Mattocks were swung at my head. Was I wrong, pockmarked man? Was I welcome after all?"

His blotched skin grew flushed. He looked away.

"We treated you badly," Dam Alice said. "We're very sorry. But you can come back now, as Bertram said. And anyone else you bring to help us, they'll be welcome too. Cosham will open its doors, and its granaries. You'll be fed. Sheltered."

"Loved," the short man said. Dwarf. The dwarf. That is the word I was looking for.

"Loved," Dam Alice agreed.

"Interesting," I said. "You want me to find others, then? Other champions to fight for you?"

"Well," the big man said. "You can't lay siege to a castle all by yourself." He laughed, a little nervously.

I thought about that. As I was thinking, I ate what was left of the dead bird, gulping it down my throat in one go. It took a long time to go down. When I was first alive, I would have choked to death before I swallowed it all. I'm stronger now, though, and while breathing is a comfort to me sometimes, it doesn't feel as important as it used to.

"No," I said. "You're right. I can't do that alone. There'll need to be more of us."

"Then you'll help!" Dam Alice brought her hands together and squeezed them tight, her face twisted and crumpled by a hope so unexpected it came close to pain.

"I think I remember Ebberlin, when he was a boy," I said. "He killed Garian's dog with an arrow, and laughed about it."

The dwarf looked uncertain. "Aren't *you* Garian?" he asked me.

That's a mistake a lot of people make. I shook my head. "I'm what Garian became after he lay in the ground for a year. Let me think on it. I don't like Ebberlin much, and I did like living in a house. Perhaps I'll help you."

The big man drew himself up, and looked at the other two each in turn, as if to say he spoke for all of them. "We need more than a perhaps," he said.

"But that's what you're getting," I told him.

They went away, then. I saw that the dwarf was lame.

I went to the river, and called out to Peter.

"Ho, hey, harum," I called. "Boy of rainfall, boy of tears. River's son and flood's favourite, come at my beseeching."

Who needs to cross these waters? Peter answered. He had not yet shown himself.

"Nobody yet," I said. "It's me, that used to be Garian. I came to talk, is what."

The water of the lake rose up in a great spume, that shaped itself into a boy. He skimmed across the surface the way a ripple does, breaking apart and coming together ever and again, until he stood before me.

Ho, Once-Was-Garian, and hey, he said. *What is it you'd talk about?*

"An offer was put to me," I said, and I told him what it was.

Well, Peter said, *whelming Errencester is a fine idea. I hate them all, in that castle, because of what they did to Magrete in the time when I was alive. But your siege will fail. Those gates won't open to you, and Uther's walls can't be made to fall.*

"It's not Uther any more, it's Ebberlin. And as for the walls, I have a plan. Will you come with me, and help me?"

I cannot. I stand in the torrent and take its toll. I can't come on dry land again.

"I know it. How if the land were not dry, though?"

What?

"How if there was a great storm, with sheets of rain coming down? Could you not run from drop to drop to drop, and so come out of the water and onto the earth without taking hurt?"

Peter was silent for a long while. He let himself fall back into the spate, and came back a moment later in a new shape, thinner and taller. *I have no idea if that would work*, he said.

"Would you like to try?"

With all my heart, if it means vengeance on Uther's kin. But will we go together?

"That's my plan."

And breach the keep that never yet was broken?

"Even so."

But… must we wait for a storm, then? There are not many in the dead winter.

"Leave that to me. I know a way to bring one."

Morjune was twelve years old when she was taken as a witch and burned.

It was all done very properly, and according to the law. The villagers of Cosham put her in Fra Nuggle's barn, tied to a metal stake that they had hammered into the floor there. They waited for the circuit magistrate to come through, and set her before him, charging that she had blighted Fra Nuggle's crops and caused his wife to deliver a welter of blood instead of a live baby.

The evidence was strong. Did Morjune not live alone in her dead mother's house? And had she not missed going to church three Sundays out of every month? And did she not mutter to herself when she walked, as if she were talking to a devil nobody else could see?

The circuit magistrate, a man who had learned his law in far-off Oxford, put Morjune to very thorough question. After her thumbs and fingers were crushed with a screw and half her teeth were drawn out with pliers, the girl admitted that she was indeed a witch and had done all the things that were alleged against her.

She was burned in the village square, and since it was a market day a good crowd came to watch her die.

Her coming back was a great deal quieter. Nobody realised she was there at all until Dam Alice noticed there was a lamp burning in old Mother Jessop's house, which with Morjune's death should by rights be empty. After she reported this three nights in a row, some men went to the house to see for themselves what was what.

There was no lamp. Morjune was there, and she was still on fire. It was not a blameful fire, though. It ran across the floor of the old house, and climbed the walls, and licked at the table and chairs, but none of those things were consumed. Morjune sat in the kitchen corner, with her knees drawn up to her chest, and offered no harm to anyone.

The village priest, Father Hasting, exorcised her with prayers and holy water, but she only came back. He tried again, with bell and book and candle, to no better effect. After that, the villagers left Morjune alone and she did them the same courtesy. She wanted no further argument with them.

She wanted none with me, either, and wouldn't come out at first when I went to her house and sat down at her table. After a while, though, when I didn't speak or move, she toppled a pot off the kitchen stove, and then a trencher off the bench, and then a chair.

"Go away," she whispered. Her voice was like the skittering of small beasts in dry leaves.

"I will, soon," I said. "Morjune, the people of the village have asked me to whelm the castle of Errencester and kill Duke Ebberlin. They say they'll give me, and everyone that goes with me, a home and a welcome thereafter."

"I've already got a home. I live here."

"But nobody speaks to you. Nobody comes."

"That's how I like it."

"God give you grace, then. If you're never lonely, and never bored, they've nothing to give you and nor have I."

We were both of us quiet a while after that. "What would you want me for?" Morjune asked at last. "I'm only a ghost. And my fire's only a memory of fire. It doesn't burn."

"I don't want you for that, but for another trick entirely."

"I'm not a witch, revenant boy. I never was. I only said that so they'd stop hurting me."

"I know how torture works, Morjune."

"So did they. What trick would you have me do?"

I told her what was in my mind. The flames came creeping around me as I talked, and climbed the legs of the table, and danced upon its top. When I left, the whole house was burning, the fire roaring like a wild animal as it leapt from floor to beams to thatch and up into the sky, as if it were going home to the sun, the fount of all fires.

Just as it did every night, to no end or avail.

❖

The villagers sent the dwarf to tell me that they were not happy with me. His name, I learned, was Thomas. That had been my mother's father's name.

"It's the witch," he said. "Morjune." He threw out his arms in a kind of shrug, as if he were casting the words on the ground between us, showing at the same time his empty hands. Showing how far he was from intending harm. "Master Bertram and Dam Alice never meant for you to consort with fiends and damned souls."

I was sitting on the parapet of the village well, talking with Peter who was down in the water below me. I had gone first to my mother and father's house, but my father's brother, Benjemin, was living there now with his children, and they all screamed at the sight of me.

Did they not know me? Had they not heard the story? Apparently not.

"Damned souls," I said back to him. "Is that what she is?"

"She was condemned for black magic. You can't do such things and go to Heaven."

"She didn't go to Heaven, though, did she? Or to Hell, either. She came here, to Cosham. I think we can agree that's in between."

Thomas frowned, and scratched his elbow. He looked to be working through my words to see if there was any chink or hole in them. "It may be that Master Bertram and Dam Alice are right," I said, "and angels will get the job done faster. Tell them to send me some. Until then, I'll work with what I've got."

❖

Unsung Jill should have been the easiest of all to recruit. A corpse-candle is best to summon her with, but an ordinary tallow candle will do, and being a bogyar she delights in mischief for its own sake. But when I called her name and pinched the wick to put out the light, she didn't come. I was alone in the dark.

I'll try again later, I thought, and went to talk with Kel and Anna in the Crowfell woods. We were friends of a long time, and comfortable with one another. I found them feeding on a deer they'd brought down together. They invited me to share the meal, but I thanked them kindly and said no. Kel's appetite is huge, when he's hairy, and a deer splits two ways more easily than three.

When they had eaten their fill, I told them about the plan to whelm Errencester. They were delighted, and said they would be pleased to come along and help so long as the moon was full. "What about Magrete, though?" Kel said.

"I have a plan for Magrete."

"I wouldn't wish to hurt her."

"No. Nor would I. My plan's not that."

"If we come to the keep and can't breach it, it will go hard with us."

"I warrant you, we'll crack the walls as if Errencester were a new-laid egg."

They liked the sound of that, and renewed their promises. There had to be a full moon, which gave me two days yet to finish my preparations. In truth, I was all but done. The main thing now was to treat with Unsung

Jill. Without her help I couldn't do anything. She was like the nail that made the horse throw its shoe in the old story, and caused the king to fall and the battle to be lost. She would bring the storm, and the storm would let Peter rise up out of the river. Or else she wouldn't, and there was nothing to be done after all.

I thought I could make her join with us, if only she would talk to me. So perhaps words were the nail.

Benjemin's oldest son, Arran, came looking for me. He found me in the broken barn behind my uncle's orchard, where I had gone because my being at the well made too many people afraid to come there and fill their buckets.

When he came to the door I stopped what I was doing, which was writing names on pieces of slate, and bid him enter.

"Are you my cousin?" he asked me. That question must have been turning in his mind ever since I came to the house. I could have said yes, or even no, but a lie told to a child is a weightier thing than one told to a grown man or woman. Children haven't come to an understanding of the world, and they may build your lies into their believing in ways that will come to hurt them.

"Come here," I said. "Sit by me. Do you know your letters?"

"No. I can count up to ten, though." He sat beside me, though his eyes as he looked at me were big and troubled. It took courage. I smiled at him. Then I remembered what I look like when I smile, and stopped.

"Your cousin Garian died," I said. "Of a fever. His

father, your uncle Hale, buried him in Viglund's Church, as he might have been expected to do. But when he and his wife, Sarah, went home, their grief did not abate. Instead it grew stronger and stronger. People who are sorrowing do foolish things, sometimes. His mother and father did something very stupid indeed. They went to Southfold. They found a wise man there, a sorcerer named Cain Caradoc, and asked him to bring their son back.

"The sorcerer knew two fools when he saw them. He said he could do it, but asked how they would pay him. They offered eight shillings, which was all they had, but though it was a fortune to them he told them it was not enough. I will bring your son back, he said, but I'll take a tithing of him for myself. You can have all of his body, and most of his soul. I'll just keep one small piece. I can use it in my magics."

Arran looked at me solemnly and fearfully. "What did they say?"

"They said yes. They'd walked all the way to Southfold, and screwed their hopes up higher with each mile they walked. To say no would have destroyed them. So the spell was made, and what came up out of the grave was me. So your question is easier to ask than it is to answer. Some of me is, or was, some of your cousin. But I'm not him, and I don't answer to his name."

Arran cast his gaze on the ground, and on the pile of slates there. He touched the pile with his foot, and the slates slid sideways. Some of them fell and broke. The boy startled. "I'm sorry!" he said. "I didn't mean to."

"It's fine," I said. "I need them broken anyway."

"Were Uncle Hale and Aunt Sarah happy when you came home to them?"

"They were not. They were struck to the heart when they saw me, and withal they were ashamed and sickened by what they'd done. My father took me into the woods a long way and tried to lose me there, but I found my way back. Then he tried to kill me, but that proved impossible. My body doesn't remember hurts the way a living body does. It finds its way back to the same shape, ever and again.

"So in the end, they gathered a few things and left in the night. I woke to an empty house – the house you live in now. I searched for them a while. And I suppose I could have found them if I'd put my mind to it. But I looked in my heart, or where I thought my heart should be, and I found I didn't care enough to chase after them. They'd made me out of love and thoughtlessness, which I suppose is how most people are made, and then they'd regretted the bargain. It happens every day."

"But then the house was yours. You could have carried on living in Cosham."

"Cosham didn't want me."

"But it does now?"

"Yes. It does now. Do you want to help me to break up these slates, now, and tell me some names to put on them."

"What kind of names?"

"Men's names. Any you can think of."

He came up with several that I hadn't thought of. Allan and Iain, Luke, Charles, Mark, Geoffrey... I wrote them all down, one by one, on the jagged shards of slate, while the dusk deepened around us, joining up the shadows in the barn.

Her presence came over me like a blanket, making the sounds of wind and birdsong and creaking wood sound dull and far away. "You'd best go home now," I said to Arran. "It's getting dark, and your mother will be looking for you."

He stood, wiping dirt from the back of his breeks. "I'm sorry for what happened to you," he said.

"It's kind of you to say so. Thank you for visiting with me, cousin. And go well."

He nodded and went scampering off, as fast as if he knew what was behind him.

"I didn't speak your name," I said to the dark.

"Yes," Unsung Jill whispered. "You did, last night, and that calling still holds. I choose when I come, and where I come, and what I look like when I come. Will you turn, fragment of a boy, and look me in the eye?"

"I'd rather not," I said. "I spent long enough in the ground. I don't wish to be dragged back there by your green eye, Jill."

"Look in the yellow one, then."

"I like that even less. Is that why you've come? To trick me and tie me up?"

The whisper of her breath went across my neck. "No," she said. And then, "I heard you talking, with the little one."

"And?"

"And I remember."

"What do you remember?"

"Something. It doesn't really matter what. You'd like a storm?"

"Oh, I would, Jill. I really would. The biggest storm this land has ever seen."

"And if I give you such a thing, incomplete child, what have you got to give me in return?"

"I can offer you what was offered to me. A home. A place to live."

I felt that cold breath again, winding over me and through me. "You know where I live."

"I know where you live now. Have you no longing for new things and places?"

Silence fell, and held for a long time. A very long time. I wanted to turn around, but couldn't. If I looked her in the eye, the best that would come would be disaster. In the end she said "You'll have your storm. Say my name again, and I'll come to you. But look you be not foresworn, little piece of a mortal child. You cannot imagine what it means to break your word to me."

A long time after, when I was sure she was gone, I set down the slate and the sliver of glass I was using to write on it. I covered my eyes with my hands, and thought of nothing. There was great warmth and comfort in nothing, right then.

They came into the barn, in the full light of noon. Perhaps they thought I would be weakest then.

"What is it you mean to do?" Dam Alice asked. Master Bertram and Thomas stood behind her. All three of them looked angry. All three of them looked afraid.

"Why, I mean to march on Errencester," I told her.

"To march? You talk as if you've got an army. You're no more than a handful!"

"But was ever such a handful scraped together, lady, since the world was made?"

She made an impatient gesture – a shrug of the head that tossed my words away. "You've leagued with things we can't countenance. Cursed things."

"Is it so? And who did the cursing, then?"

"We thought you might speak to the one that made you. Borrow a spell from him. Black magic in a righteous cause is no sin. But this…"

I stood. It was not to frighten her, but to keep her from toppling the slates. I had not minded when the boy Arran had done it, because most of the pieces still had to be broken down into smaller pieces anyway. It would be inconvenient now to lose any of the ones I'd made. "We made a bargain," I said. "It's yet to play out. Go away now, and leave me be."

"You've broken the bargain. You're outside the spirit of it."

"I think not. Go away."

They went. I thought Thomas looked back at me as if he was sorry to be a part of this. I saw again how his left leg twisted, so his body sank down and rose up again with each step.

And oh, it was such a storm. Such a storm and such a dark! Jill did us proud.

We gathered at the river's bank, near the Wythen ford, and waited. Anna was there, and Kel. "What's in your bag?" Kel asked me.

"Slates. For throwing."

"That's well. What are we waiting for?"

We were waiting for Peter, but I didn't need to answer, for just then he reared up out of the water right beside us. He stepped out onto the riverside weeds like Noah's flood with a face and a name. *I like this much*, he said. *Thank you kindly, Garian.*

"Thank Jill," I said. "She it was that squeezed the clouds, and wreaked this riot."

Unsung Jill?

"Even her."

Ah, then I like it less. For is she not of Hell?

"What's Hell, but a warm hearth and a few good companions?" Jill whispered from behind him. A shudder went through Peter, like a wave goes through the clear ocean. He said no more.

"Well, then," I said. "Let's to it."

"Have we no more strategy than that?" Anna asked.

"Our strategy is to force them off the walls and into the keep."

"And then?"

"And then we'll see."

The river and the ford were at the bottom of a steep hill called Sheep Run, and Errencester Castle stood at the top of it. As soon as we left the margin of the river we were likely to be seen, so there was little point in creeping and crawling. Instead we ran, out of the trees that had covered us and up the hill.

We were not fired on. From the battlements of Errencester, we must have looked like ragamuffins playing a game. Until, that is, Jill drew back her arm and let fling with a fireball like a tiny sun. It took a man off the wall, so quickly that he didn't even scream as he fell.

These are just sell-swords, Peter said. *Their deaths serve no-one.*

"When you sell your sword to Ebberlin," said Kel, "you know full well who'll be on the other end of it. They get no mercy from me."

They got none from me, either. I flung my slates, one by one by one. Most of them only fell on the ground, and lay there, but the ones that bore a right name, a name of one of the bowmen and spearmen on the battlements, they went straight and true to that man's heart.

They knew us for a threat, now, and answered us in kind. Their arrows fell like hail, hitting us hard. Jill and I were not troubled by them, so we went before and drew the soldiers' fire, Jill expanding to her full height to make herself an easier target. Kel and Anna ran in our shadows, and Peter walked apart. What quarrels and bolts hit him passed straight through and went on their way. And ever and anon, as we advanced, Jill spat out hate and heat and hurt in every shape and colour, opening gaps on the walls that did not fill again.

My bag being empty now, I flung it away. I was more than happy to lose the weight. Behind me, Kel changed and Anna began to dance. When the gates loomed in front of us, Jill and I stepped aside and let them pass.

Kel is a bear, when he changes. Anna is many things, and nothing. She remembers all the flesh she's ever tasted, and weaves and winds it together in ways that were never seen before. She towered over all of us, even her brother, and where he hit the gates in the middle she hit them high.

They went down. The soldiers who had been waiting behind them, to rush out on us, went down too, crushed by a handspan's thickness of old oak and a stampede of terrible shapes that was all one girl.

We were in the bailey yard now, and in greater danger than before. This space was made to be a killing ground, squeezed as it was between the outer walls and the keep. That was why we had hit the soldiers so hard, as we came. We hoped that they would fall back into the keep rather than hold their posts and fire straight down on us.

Some of them did, but some did not, and now there was no room for quarter. I ran up the walls, into the teeth of the falling arrows, and Peter ran beside me. The caked thicknesses of storm cloud above us made the narrow space between the walls as dark as night, but Jill's fireballs gave us a trail we could follow. We went among the defenders, and we heaped ruin on them. Seeing us come, a mad boy stuck full of arrows but not faltering and a boy of water who arrows could not touch, they despaired and fled at last.

All had gone as I had hoped, so far, and I had one trick left for Duke Ebberlin and his thanes. I ran ahead; not to harry the fleeing men, but to make sure they kept on running until they reached the keep.

One of them did not. A great, slope-shouldered giant strode into my path, his back bent by the weight of a club so big and heavy it looked like an uprooted tree.

As he lifted it up, he raised his head too. I saw his face.

It was a child's face. And it was weeping.

Morjune had come into Errencester from under the ground, following the ancient stream that fed its well. Peter could have done this too, if we hadn't needed him for the attack – but he couldn't have gone where Morjune went next.

Only a ghost could slide between the stones of the keep, and even a ghost could feel the force that lived there, pushing back at her. Morjune shut her eyes and struggled on, blindly, like a traveller lost in a gale. But there was no wind here, and no rain. Not even rats skittered, though she moved through spaces where rats would readily have made their nests. Errencester Keep was inviolate.

Duke Uther, in his day, had taken the nearest way to make it so. And the spell he purchased, the ritual he used, was proof against time. No doubt he thought it proof against anything.

Emerging in one of the corridors behind the great hall, Morjune was immediately lost. But the force that pushed against her gave her a clue to where she should go. It did not push evenly, from every direction, but had a home. An origin. She swam against it, rising foot by foot towards its source.

As, outside, we met our match and were gravelled.

There might have been a moment in which I could have dodged that blow. If there was, I didn't use it. I stood there on the narrow strip of stone, so astonished that I did not even think to move.

The thing's face, so innocent and yet so terrible, was split by a grimace of grief and pity.

The club took me in the ribs, and hurled me headlong off the battlements.

Under a stone slab in the great hall, Morjune found that which she sought. There was a hollow space there, about two strides long and a foot deep. In the hollow were laid the bones of a child. She could see, with her ghost-sight, the broken rib that had been sheared through when the sharp, sharp knife had pierced the child's heart.

"Magrete," Morjune whispered. "Wake up."

For a long time, nothing. Then, *Go away*, Magrete whispered. The same words Morjune had spoken to me, when I asked her to make one in this endeavour. *Go away and leave me. I'm asleep.*

"You've slept long and late. It's time to wake up."

No.

"My comrades have come to free you."

Then they've come too late.

And after that, no more words.

I landed in the courtyard with a crash that broke every bone in my body. Robust as I am, it would be some time before I could move.

I was not given that time. The thing that had struck me jumped down after me, with terrible and perfect aim. It landed in the centre of my back. The shattering of my spine, the explosion of my lungs and lights stunned me, and for a little while I ceased to be.

Then my body began to knit itself whole again. The agony of being remade in this way was greater than the blow, the fall and the crushing all together. I lay and suffered, unable to move, unable to think.

When finally my eyes opened again, or knew themselves to be open, the first thing I saw was Jill. She was lying along the ground in twisted skeins, her mouth and eyes open wide in the semblance of a scream. There was no colour in either of her eyes. Whatever power was pressing on her had drained the magics out of them and left her – for the moment – empty.

That sight was so terrible, it was many moments before I saw what lay beyond her. Kel was fighting with a man. One sole man, and yet he did not fall. He was not one of the soldiers, for he wore no armour and carried no weapon. His yellow hair whipped in the wind, untrammelled by any helmet. He seemed to need none of these things. The swipes of Kel's great, curved claws did not come near him.

But his strokes found Kel. He flexed the fingers of his hands, in tiny movements like the caresses of a lover, and Kel staggered, as if great blows battered him. A stroke, and his back was bowed. A pass, and dark blood sprayed from his broken mouth.

Some of the blood landed in a puddle, and the puddle, taking the stain of it, cried aloud in dismay. The puddle was Peter.

❖

"Magrete! Magrete, please! Talk to me."

But no. Nothing.

"Magrete, you've got to help us or my friends will fail. And if they fail you'll lie here forever!"

Still, nothing at all.

Kel was down, in a spreading pool of his own blood. Fed with the endless, stinging rain, the pool was quickly becoming a lake.

The man who bore no weapons stood over him, and raised both his hands above his head. Since all his gestures so far had been so small, and the effects so wide and terrible, I did not see how Kel would survive the bringing down of those hands.

Into that moment, Anna came. Nothing up to now had touched the man, and Anna did not succeed in touching him either. But she hit so hard, in her massy, churning shape of shapes, that the man was pushed aside ten feet or more. When his arms swept down, with the fingers of both hands spread out wide, it was only grass and mud and a few cobbles that exploded. Kel was left alive.

But now the man turned his attention to Anna, and she fared no better than her brother had. Her stinger descended like a flail, and her body bore on him like a ship's anchor flung down, but nothing would do. We were dying, each and all, and there was nothing we could do. The blond man was proof against the strongest of us. And still the monster with the child's face tore and pulled at me, rendering what was left of me into smaller and smaller pieces.

It came to me then, though, as my body surrendered perforce to this dissolution, that I had seen hair of such a bright colour once before. It had been a great many years ago, but the occasion had been memorable. A man like this had stood by when I was raised up out of the earth and made – after a fashion – to live again.

Was it possible that this man and that other were not two, but one? That this was Cain Caradoc, the sorcerer who had taken out a piece of my soul as the price of my second birth?

It was possible, I decided. And if it was possible, other things might be possible too. There was, after all, very little left to lose.

Morjune began to sing.

She sang a song that is sometimes called *I Will Tell You One-oh*. The Jews sing it, and the Christians likewise, and each believes they invented it. It's taught to children to make them remember their numbers, and the theme is call and answer.

> *I will tell you one-oh.*
> *One is God in Heaven-oh.*
> *I will tell you two-oh.*
> *Two is the blameless babes, and one is God in Heaven-oh.*
> *I will tell you three-oh.*
> *Three went in the furnace, two is the blameless babes and one is God in Heaven-oh.*
> *I will tell you four-oh.*
> *Four the gospel creatures, three went in the furnace, two is the blameless babes and one is God in Heaven-oh.*

And so on, for as long as you can count. Morjune knew it all the way up to thirteen, and so she sang. Then she began again at one.

Stop it! Magrete wailed at last. *Stop singing! I'm trying to sleep.*

"Sleep later, lazy girl. For now, you have to listen. I'm Morjune, the witch. Well, that's what they call me. I was killed before my time, just like you were, though they killed me out of fear and you out of cunning and policy. We should be friends, you and I."

No. Leave me be. I don't have any friends.

"You did have, once."

No.

"When you were alive, I mean."

No.

"There was the boy, Peter. He loved you well."

A silence.

I thought he would come for me. I waited. He never came.

"Oh, but he did. Small as he was, he hammered on the gate of Errencester and defied the lords inside. He called them cowards, and murderers, to seal their castle safe against siege and sundering with a maiden sacrifice. He laid such names on them, it made the men blush and the women weep."

Another silence.

And then what?

"They scored him with whips, and broke him with cudgels. And afterwards they threw him, weighted with stones, into Kirkul River, where he has bided ever since. But now, this very day, he comes again."

He is here? Peter is here?

"He's in the castle, but not in the keep. He can't come to you, Magrete, because of the spell they made all those long years ago. The spell they wove out of your murder."

A third silence. But this one was different from the other two.

Tell him, Magrete whispered.

Tell him I'm coming.

I closed my eyes. Actually just one eye, the other having been plucked out of my head.

I closed my ears to Anna's screams. Even now, they were screams of wrath as much as of pain. Cut and crushed and drawn though she was, she would not fall – because if she fell, she would leave Kel's body undefended.

I closed every sense but one. I could not taste my blood. I could not feel my pain, or the chill rain as it fell on me. Nothing was left inside my head but me.

And – I hoped, I prayed – the *other* me.

If the flax-haired man was truly Cain Caradoc, then his monster might well be the piece he took from me. I would not have known its face. A few glimpses in mirrors and meres, many a year and gone, had left no sense of what I was. I only knew the beast that assailed me bore a child's face, and therefore had had a child, or a part of a child, in its making.

I reached out to it.

And found it.

And drew it into me.

The sorcerer felt the change at once. He forgot his attack on Anna and turned to face me. I mean, he turned with that intention, but I was already too big. He faced my twisted thigh, my splintered leg, the bones of my calf and shin as they folded themselves back into my swelling, towering body.

Cain Caradoc had claimed such a tiny part of me for his use, but the magics he had worked with it had been vast beyond imagining. And now I was opening the rest of myself to those same magics. I burgeoned like a tree, a century's growth packed into a few wild seconds.

"*Per potestatem—*" the sorcerer bellowed. I swung my fist and he soared, arse over head, across the bailey yard. A wall stopped his flight, and his abominations, forever more, though in truth my mighty hand had already crushed him into ruin.

I'm here, Magrete cried, in all our ears. *I'm with you. Oh, I'm with you! Where is Peter?*

Peter was spilled on the ground and too weak to answer her, but she knew him anyway and flung herself on him, into him, greedy for the touch of the one that had ever loved her best.

So now the spell that kept the keep from harm was broken. A maiden's sacrifice was the recipe, a maiden's soul the vital, secret thing that bound the stones together stronger than mortar. Until the maiden woke, and knew herself, and left the keep.

I struck the walls with my hands, again and again. When the stones began to crumble, I pushed my fingers in between them and wrenched at them to widen the gap. It was hard work, but by and by Jill came up on my left-hand side and Anna on my right, and the three of us went at it with a will.

Inside the walls, like the meat inside a nut, we found Duke Ebberlin and his thanes, his wife and her serving wenches, a few counsellors, merchants and parasites, a few cooks and vassals, and another score or so of soldiers.

Anna ate the Duke, and Jill despatched his lady. She was a sorceress, too, but she had only journeyman skills and could not command a power as old as our Jilly's.

The soldiers had lost all heart by this time, and tried to run away. We should have let them go, but we were in a blood rage and killed them to the last man. Kel and Anna ate a great many of them, which is a hard way to die. Others looked Jill in the eye, which is harder still. The ones I squeezed and twisted and broke with my house-sized hands probably had the best of it.

Peter was himself again, by this time, and called us to a halt – berating us, besides, for taking out our anger on men who had no hope of hurting us. The battle being won, he said, what we were doing now was only slaughter.

And much more to the same tune, until we came back to ourselves and submitted again to the reins of reason. We allowed the survivors to go forth unmolested, only enjoining them never again to return to Errencester, or Cosham village, or the demesnes round about, on pain of the death they had escaped that day.

"What now?" Jill asked.

And it says much that she asked it. For she had lived ten thousand years, and a thousand more, and never needed to weigh one course against another until that day.

"Now," I said, "we take our reward."

"That's not what was meant!" the man Bertram protested. He had to shout to bring his words to where my ears were, because I was still as tall as a tower. That was intentional. I wanted there to be no mistaking the seriousness of our purpose.

"It's what was said," I told him. "You promised us a home."

"But Errencester Castle is the strongest keep in the county! It was ever the dwelling of this land's lord. If you stay in it—"

"We've no interest in ruling you. But we don't much care to live with you, either. Some of us have been down that road before, and it didn't end well for us."

"Armies will come," the woman warned. "As moths come to a flame."

I smiled. "And they'll fare as well as moths do, when they come to a flame."

They made more noise, but nothing to the purpose. They had meant to petition the Lord Howard or the Count Tremegne, or this one or that one, and by offering Errencester up as a kind of bride-price to have a sweeter and a longer honeymoon. But that did not fit with our design, and we gave it no thought.

We were a family now. We were a seven, and so we meant to stay, until the waters below and the waters above held congress again and the whole green Earth was whelmed.

G.V. Anderson
www.gvanderson.com

Simon Avery
www.simonaveryblog.wordpress.com

M.R. Carey
www.facebook.com/MRCareyAuthor

Paul M. Feeney
www.twitter.com/PaulMichaels75

Tim Lebbon
www.timlebbon.net

Alison Littlewood
www.alisonlittlewood.co.uk

Maura McHugh
www.splinister.com

Priya Sharma
www.priyasharmafiction.wordpress.com

Phil Sloman
www.insearchofperdition.blogspot.com

Catriona Ward
www.facebook.com/catrionawardauthor

Ren Warom
www.renwaromsumwelt.wordpress.com

blackshuckbooks.co.uk

Also available:

GREAT BRITISH HORROR 1:
GREEN AND PLEASANT LAND

FEATURING STORIES BY

JASPER BARK

A.K. BENEDICT

RAY CLULEY

JAMES EVERINGTON

RICH HAWKINS

V.H. LESLIE

LAURA MAURO

ADAM MILLARD

DAVID MOODY

SIMON KURT UNSWORTH

BARBIE WILDE

GREAT BRITISH HORROR 2:
DARK SATANIC MILLS

FEATURING STORIES BY

CHARLOTTE BOND

PAUL FINCH

ANDREW FREUDENBERG

GARY FRY

CATE GARDNER

CAROLE JOHNSTONE

PENNY JONES

GARY MCMAHON

MARIE O'REGAN

JOHN LLEWELLYN PROBERT

ANGELA SLATTER

GREAT BRITISH HORROR 3:
FOR THOSE IN PERIL

FEATURING STORIES BY

STEPHEN BACON

SIMON BESTWICK

GEORGINA BRUCE

KAYLEIGH MARIE EDWARDS

JOHNNY MAINS

PAUL MELOY

THANA NIVEAU

ROSALIE PARKER

KIT POWER

GUY N. SMITH

DAMIEN ANGELICA WALTERS